Dear Reader,

Like Lucy Willows's road to discovery in *Just Fly Away*, Andrew McCarthy's road to writing Lucy's story was anything but a straight line. A successful film, TV, and stage actor from a very young age and then a director, Andrew later became a travel writer, documenting his trips across the globe for national publications and in a best-selling travel memoir. Then, when he first sat down to create a novel, he thought it would be for an adult readership. It wasn't until fifteen-year-old Lucy Willows's voice came to him — as it happens, on a long airplane trip — that Andrew understood his career would take him in yet another direction, as a writer of young adult fiction.

Like her creator, Lucy Willows is a thinker and a seeker, and travel is at the heart of her story. Lucy captured me with her refreshing directness. While fictional plots so often turn on what's not said or asked, Lucy plunges headfirst into the big, difficult questions. But befitting her creator's own history, Lucy's literal route and her surroundings are as essential as her interior voyage to her self-discovery. From her backyard picnic table to the Jersey shore to a road trip through New York City and Boston on the way to the lobster shacks and lighthouses of the rocky Maine coast, Andrew McCarthy brings Lucy and her journey to vivid, aching, joyful life.

And now, lucky reader, Lucy's path is about to cross your own. Have a great trip!

Elise Howard
Publisher, Algonquin Young Readers

JUST FLY AWAY

JUST
FLY
AWAY

ANDREW McCARTHY

ALGONQUIN 2017

Published by
ALGONQUIN YOUNG READERS
an imprint of Algonquin Books of Chapel Hill
Post Office Box 2225
Chapel Hill, North Carolina 27515-2225

a division of
WORKMAN PUBLISHING
225 Varick Street
New York, New York 10014

© 2017 by Andrew McCarthy.
All rights reserved.
Printed in the United States of America.
Published simultaneously in Canada by Thomas Allen & Son Limited.
Design by TK.

LIBRARY OF CONGRESS CATALOGING-IN-PUBLICATION DATA

[TK]

10 9 8 7 6 5 4 3 2 1
First Edition

Dedication TK

JUST FLY AWAY

1

I SUPPOSE IF I THOUGHT ABOUT IT I would have to say that I had a premonition when we were down the shore that something bad was going to happen. That's not as bizarre as it might sound. I get these feelings sometimes. They come at strange moments.

A couple of times a year the whole family piles into the car and we cruise down the Parkway to go to the boardwalk on the shore and play a little Skee-Ball and take a spin on the Tilt-A-Whirl—stuff like that. If it's late enough in the summer we go swimming. The day is always a guaranteed crowd-pleaser.

"I just love breathing in that sea air," my mother must

say five or six times every visit. My sister, Julie, is very good at that pop-the-balloons-with-the-darts game, and my dad is generally pretty jolly and outgoing. This time it only took him until we were walking away from Steaks Unlimited to bring up his famous/infamous Jersey shore story.

"Did I ever tell you guys about the summer after I graduated high school and I worked as a dishwasher a few blocks from here—"

"At the Pizza Pub!" Julie blared out.

"You only told us fifty times, Dad," I said.

"We love when you remind us of that, darling," my mom said. Then she paused for a large bite of her sandwich. "Every time."

"All right, all right," my dad groaned. Frankly, there really wasn't much more to the story than that.

Everyone was strolling down the boardwalk scarfing various greasy goodies—I was eating those famous cheese balls, Julie and my dad were splitting a Philly cheesesteak. And my mom was having one of the famous sausage sandwiches—down the shore is the only time I ever see my mother eat what she would normally call "crap."

Julie then spied an arcade that had one of those machines with the silver claw that drops down and tries to pick things up. She spent considerable financial resources going after this ridiculous-looking hat. She came close a few times.

Later, when she and I came back from a double go on

that spinning swing ride—which I'll admit is very childish but sort of a tradition of ours—my dad was standing in the sun waiting with that hat in his hand, beaming with pride.

"It only took him ten tries," my mom said. She put her arm around his waist.

"Hey!" His voice sounded all fake offended. "It was only nine."

He handed Julie the hat, then held something out toward me. "And I thought you might like this, young lady."

It was a small furry thing, an inch or two long, attached to a little chain.

"What is it?" I asked.

"You don't know what this is?" my father said. He shook his head sadly—my dad was really a very bad actor. "You have led a very sheltered life— we have got to get to the shore more often. This is a lucky rabbit's foot. I won it for you at that pound-the-frog game."

"What's it do?"

"It doesn't *do* anything. You put it in your pocket and carry it around and it brings you good luck."

I actually liked the idea a lot and went to put it in my pocket.

"Gross," Julie said.

My hand froze. "Is it from a real rabbit?" I asked.

"Of course not, Lucy," my mother said.

I stuffed it in my jeans.

Shortly after that, I had my weird premonition. I was

standing with Julie, waiting for her to buy cotton candy—
the appeal of which I have never understood. I looked over
at my mom and dad, who were nearby, leaning against
the boardwalk railing and looking out at the ocean, still a
murky greenish gray this early in the year, when I got an
uneasy sort of feeling.

I can never usually put my finger on exactly what's
wrong when this happens; it's just this weird sensation that
I get right between my shoulder blades—like the shivers,
but not quite. That's my spot, between my shoulder blades—
it's my Achilles' heel. It's a feeling I definitely don't like, so I
generally try to keep my guard up.

After what seemed like a few minutes, but was probably
only a few seconds, the feeling went away. By the second
time we rode the Pirates Plunge, I had forgotten all about
it. The day wore on. We looked at the weirdos shuffling
down the boardwalk, we played too many arcade games,
and late in the afternoon we walked on the beach and put
our feet in the freezing water. When the sun started to sink
over Buffies Baby Burgers, we headed north.

As usual, my dad inflicted his classic rock radio station
on us all, which, I have to admit, plays some catchy tunes,
but only if cranked up to an extremely high volume. And
so, as the sky grew dark and the exits flew by, the entire car
belted out a song about a small-town girl and the smell of
wine and cheap perfume and something that went on and

on and on and on, and then another one about tramps with hot cars that were born to run.

If I'm to speak truthfully, this happy little tale of family bliss was not entirely uncommon; we generally had a good time together—but this was to be the last one. The last one B.T.—Before Thomas. Before Julie and I found out our father had been lying to us for more or less our entire lives.

That happened the next day.

2

MY MOTHER LIKES TO SAY that I'm a pessimist. I am not a pessimist. I'm just not getting too excited or raising my hopes too high, so that when something bad happens I won't be disappointed, I'll be ready for it.

But I wasn't ready for this. Not at all.

Or the way I found out, all of a sudden like that, after dinner, without warning. Then once I knew it, that was it, I couldn't not know it ever again.

It was a complete shock. Complete shock. For both my sister and me. Or at least it was for me. Julie didn't act too shocked, but you can never tell what she's thinking.

We had just finished dinner out back—the first outdoor

meal of the season. The weekend had been unseasonably warm for April—that's the phrase they always use, isn't it, *unseasonably warm*. The meal had been entirely pleasant. We had spicy shrimp on skewers, which I adored. Everyone liked them a lot, but my mom made them more often than she might otherwise because of my very vocal passion for them. Now, however, those tangy crustaceans will forever be associated with this horrible evening.

Julie had talked a lot—for Julie—about her school play, and we even had some laughs at my dad's expense.

"The show is in two weeks?" he asked my sister.

"Here we go," my mom said with a smirk. My dad can't remember anything without writing it in his appointment calendar. He gets a lot of grief for it.

"Next week, Dad," Julie said.

"We'll be there," he promised her. He nodded his head, as if lodging vital information he would take with him to his grave. "So what's in two weeks?"

"Really, darling?" My mom shook her head. She was sort of grinning, but maybe not entirely. "And you're not even close to fifty yet."

"Oh, right," he said, "it's our wedding anniversary." He saved himself by giving my mom one of his winning smiles, where he squints his baby blues at her.

After the meal, Julie and I cleared the table. Which, frankly, is a pain when we eat outside. Everything has to be carried to and from the kitchen. It's the main reason

I don't like eating out there, that and the bugs. When we finally were done, Julie ran up to her room to listen to her musicals, like she always does after dinner. I was about to put on the dishwasher, but when I opened the door to the cabinet under the sink and shook the detergent box, it was empty. This drives me crazy. For some reason my mother puts stuff like empty milk and OJ cartons back all the time, so you don't know that you're out of something until you pick up the carton, and then it's too late. For years I have been telling her to just throw it out so there's no box there and that way we'll know we need to get more. It falls on deaf ears. In any case, there was no dishwasher powder.

I started to walk to the back door to tell my parents. It's one of those doors where the top and the bottom can open separately; they're called Dutch doors. Or so I'm told. I wouldn't really know, of course, having never been to Holland. The top half, with the windowpanes, was closed, secured by the brass triangle thing.

I could see my parents sitting around the table on the deck under the big pine tree, or evergreen tree, or whatever kind of tree it is. My mom was facing away from me; her feet were up on the rung of the chair my sister had been sitting in. She had her glass of wine in her hand—like she always does in the evening. She was saying something to my dad. He looked kind of surprised by whatever it was, though not in a bad way, just slightly confused. When I opened the door I heard her say, "And I think you'd be proud of him."

My father, who should have seen me right over my mom's shoulder, didn't.

"Proud of who?" I asked.

My mother pulled her feet off the chair, like I was the school principal coming into a room. My dad coughed in a weird way, as if he had suddenly choked on something he hadn't eaten.

"Nothing, sweetheart," my mom said. She was nervous as she turned her head over her shoulder in my direction, but didn't really look at me. "Nobody."

My dad's knee started bouncing up and down.

"Not nobody—obviously," I said. "Dad would be proud of who?"

"Just someone from work," my mom said.

She was lying. This made me really mad. It also scared me for some reason.

"Bullshit," I said. I'm generally not that into cursing. Of course, I went through the typical phase of swearing a lot when I was a few years younger, the way kids of a certain age do, but at this point I'm just not that into proclaiming that everything is a load of manure. This one just escaped.

"Lucy!" my dad said.

"You'd be proud of who?" I asked again, louder. I don't know why I wanted to know so badly. I didn't really care that much at first, but when they started acting so secretive, it made me kind of crazy. My father was looking at my mother. His eyebrows were raised, like he was asking her a question. I couldn't see my mother's face.

"I'm exhausted by it," my father said, with a big sigh.

"Exhausted by what?" I said.

"It's up to you," my mother said to my father.

The wind had started to blow and the tree branches above were creaking and groaning like they might break. That tree poking up through the deck has some very heavy branches and there is a lot of action when the wind blows. It provides a lot of shade, so you're not forced to sit in the blazing sun, but honestly, I am not a huge fan.

My dad was looking up at those branches.

"Exhausted by what?" I said again.

"Go and get your sister," my father said.

"Tell me what's going on." I wasn't budging.

"Lower your voice," my father said. "Go and get your sister and I will tell you both."

My mother finally turned all the way around and looked at me. Her face was really calm. It freaked me out. I backed away a few steps and then I bolted into the house. I ran through the kitchen and the living room, and then I was up the stairs and throwing open my sister's door. I walked over and killed the power button on her music.

"Hey!" she shouted.

"Mom and Dad want us out back. Now."

When we walked back out onto the deck, my parents hadn't moved. My mother had turned back away from the door, facing my father. My dad was staring straight ahead, just past my mother. I wasn't even sure he had noticed us come back out until he spoke.

"Sit down, girls," he said.

We went around the table and sat in the same spots we always do—my dad was on my left, my mom on my right, my sister across from me.

Then he told us.

"There's a child," my father said. He made a point of looking first at me and then my sister in the eye as he continued. "A boy. An eight-year-old boy. He lives here in town, with his mother. And I'm his father."

Then things got really strange. It was exactly like on those cheesy reality shows when they "re-create" things. There's a car accident in the remote woods, or there's a person on an operating table, something like that. Suddenly the person leaves his or her body and floats up to the ceiling and watches everything from above. They see the emergency team operate on them down below in a desperate race to keep them from going to the light and remain instead among the humanity of this plane and all the suffering and heartache of this sorrowful world. The heroic doctor calls for the scalpel and says things like "We're losing her, more suction."

That's what happened to me the second my dad told us he had another kid. Up I went.

Maybe because I was floating, I wasn't sure I even understood what my dad was saying. It didn't seem to make any sense. I knew what the words meant, but I couldn't compute them. My dad had another child? Who we didn't know? Living in our town?

After a while my sister said, "Oh"—which could have won the Academy Award for understatement of the century.

My mother and father sort of chuckled a little at that, but there was nothing funny going on.

"What's his name?" my sister asked.

"His name is Thomas," my father said.

"How old is he?" she asked.

He had just said that. What was the matter with her? But at that moment I probably wouldn't have been able to tell you how old he was either.

"He's eight," my father repeated. A little more than half my age. This kid had been alive for most of my life?

"What's he like?" Julie asked. She sounded like a robot. Why all these questions?

"Well," my father said, "I don't really know him very well. We don't have much contact. That's the way his mother wants it."

Suddenly I was slammed back into my body. "You have another family?" I blurted.

"No, Lucy," my mother said.

I snapped my head around to her. "Let *him* tell me."

My parents looked at each other.

"No, Lucy," my father said slowly. "I don't have another family. I had a child with another woman, but we don't have much contact, any contact at all, really. Those are her wishes. They live in town. Occasionally I run into her. It was something that happened a long time ago, so no, we don't see each other—or talk very often. But there is a child."

Nobody moved a muscle, not for a long time.

"And all this happened after you were married to Mom," I finally said, stating the obvious.

"Yes," my father said.

You hear about the parents of some girl just like me getting divorced all the time. Then eventually you discover that one of them had been screwing around and the mom found out and there was crying and screaming and throwing the dad out and then the kids are shuttled back and forth, just like you always figured in the back of your mind that they would be, because everyone gets divorced in the end anyway, right? But this kid situation added an extra twist to it, that's for sure. So what the hell was my mother still doing with him?

"Did you know about this?" I stared at her. "When did you find out?"

"Your father told me several years ago."

"Several *years*?"

"Yes, Lucy," she said.

"How many years, exactly?"

"About five years ago."

"Five years!" I heard my voice, and it was shrieking. I didn't mean for it to be, but there was not much I could do about it. My palms were sweating.

"And you just sit there like that?" I shouted at her.

"Lucy," my father said, "be respectful to your mother."

"Why? You weren't."

"Okay, Lucy. That's enough," my mom said.

"I can't believe this. Dad screws some woman, has a kid, who we don't even know about for most of our lives, and we're all supposed to just sit here? Have you even met him?" I was staring at my mother.

"I've known who they are for some time. I ran into him and his mother today. He's a lovely boy, and that's what I was telling your father when you came out."

How could she be saying these things? What the hell was going on? I looked over at Julie. She was just staring off into space. She was no help at all, as usual.

"Are we finished?" I said.

"Lucy, it's a lot to take in. Why don't we talk about it for a while," my mother said, finishing her glass of wine.

"There's nothing to talk about."

"Lucy—" My mother's voice was very soft now.

"What, Mom? What?" My voice was not soft. I couldn't stop shrieking. "Why don't you just have another glass of Chablis and forget about it. What else is new?"

"Lucy, don't talk to your mother like that, do you hear me?"

"No. Fuck you, Dad! You don't tell me what to do." I'd never said that to either one of them before. A milestone. I shoved my chair back hard across the deck. One of the big rules in our house was to always lift the outdoor chairs and not push them so that the wood didn't get ruined. I didn't care. My chair made a harsh scraping sound—I saw later that it had dug deep grooves into the wood that will never be gone.

Up in my room I paced around—I didn't know what to do. I wanted to break everything. I felt like a giant fool for some reason. What else didn't I know? Were we adopted, too? Were we aliens from Mars? If I hadn't walked in on them at that instant, when exactly would my parents have gotten around to sharing this little bit of minor information? Who even were those people at my dinner table?

I caught a look at my less than satisfying image in the mirror above the dresser, which made me feel even worse. You hear all this talk about how great curly hair is, but I'd give anything to have my brown mop be straight and silky. That Thomas kid probably had shiny, wavy hair. He probably didn't have my puffy cheeks, either. And he certainly didn't inherit my mother's brown eyes, now did he?

When I flopped down on my bed, something in my pocket jabbed me. I jumped back up. It was the lucky rabbit's foot my dad had given me down the shore the day before. It had been bulky in my pants all day long but I kept it in there because my dad had said it was good luck, and up until now I'd always given my father the benefit of the doubt.

When I yanked it out of my pocket, I saw what had stabbed me. Beneath the fur near the tip there were four claws. How had I not noticed this before? How could I not have known?

I opened my window that looked out over the front lawn and flung the thing as hard as I could.

Some luck.

3

THERE ARE JUST SO MANY unsettling possibilities about life that you can't be on guard for them all. Things will be going along fine—not extraordinary or fantastic, just normal, regular—and then something like this happens and nothing is normal anymore, and it won't ever be normal again. There is nothing you can do about it. Absolutely nothing. And even though this kind of thing might happen to anyone, it's still a big deal when it happens to you.

After I chucked the rabbit's foot, I stood at the window, staring out. I couldn't see where it had landed. By this time the streetlamp by the curb had come on. My mother's voice came from downstairs, moving through the house in my direction. That's all I needed. The wind blew in against my face. I climbed out onto the narrow catwalk that wraps around the second-story windows. I had never been out there before, or even thought about it. My sister's window was about fifteen feet away. To get there I had to crouch under some branches of a big tree with red leaves. As I was ducking under them, I grabbed the largest branch and swung myself up over the catwalk's railing, out above the yard.

The branch bent hard and fast under my full weight, and I went swooping down toward the ground, about twenty feet below. Before I landed, the branch stripped through my hand and went flying back up. Leaves rained down; my palm and fingers got scraped pretty badly. I hit the ground hard. A sharp pain shot through my ankle and up my leg as I tried to stand. I didn't care. I got to my feet and tore out of the yard.

For no good reason I was headed toward the 7-Eleven, the generic haven for aimless teenagers throughout America. Luckily, it was only three blocks from my house. The sky was almost completely dark by the time I got there. Inside things were very bright, no shadows anywhere. Not in a 7-Eleven. My ankle was getting worse by the second. I looked down to see if it was bleeding or if the bone might be sticking out of my skin, but it was just swollen like a grapefruit, and really red. When I touched it, it was as if my finger were a hot knife. I grabbed a can of Coke and hobbled to the counter. Only after I placed it in front of the really overweight guy behind the register did I realize that I had no money. I didn't even bother to explain—I just left it there and limped out of the store.

As I staggered back across the parking lot toward home, my ankle was hurting so much that I had to sit down on one of those cement bumps meant to stop cars from over-shooting parking spaces.

I didn't have anything with me, no cash, no phone, nothing. I was helpless, useless. Then I was bawling my eyes out. My chest was heaving and my shoulders were shaking, and I couldn't catch my breath. My ankle hurt, I couldn't get a simple Coke, and my dad apparently had some secret kid stashed across town.

It was like this bad movie where the poor main char-acter discovered she had been switched at birth and wasn't supposed to be a pauper after all, but was really the child of a rich family. After living at the fancy home for a little while, she realized that the destitute family loved her and that's what was more important. Except in my case the big surprise turned out to be that my father was someone I didn't know at all. And was a total liar.

I cried for a long time in that parking lot. I might still be crying if someone hadn't eventually tapped my shoulder. It was the guy from the 7-Eleven, standing behind me with the can of Coke in his hand.

"You can pay tomorrow," he said, reaching the Coke out

toward me. "It's no big deal. I won't tell my boss. It's nothing to cry about. It's just a Coke."

I felt really bad that I'd thought about how fat he was when I was inside.

"Thanks," I said.

He put the can on the cement thing next to me, then turned and went back to his life.

I pressed the icy cold can against my ankle for a few seconds, then I cracked the lid and took a sip. It tasted super sweet, perhaps one of the top three Cokes I've ever had. Good old reliable Coke, you could always count on it to do the job.

Cars were going by and I watched their lights zip past as I drank. *It must be nice to be going somewhere*, I thought.

I'd almost forgotten about my ankle, but now it started to throb again. When my Coke was done, I crunched the can and managed to stand. I had to put all my weight on my left leg. My right ankle couldn't take any pressure at all. I tossed the can toward the garbage dumpster a few feet away and missed, naturally. I started to go toward it but my ankle was so bad that I couldn't even bend to get it. I hate littering; it pisses me off. But what could I do, I was helpless in the situation. I left it there.

The walk back took forever. A half block from home I saw Mr. Schmitz across the street in the dark, walking Josie. All I needed was to have that yappy little mongrel spot me and go crazy like she always does. I hid behind a large tree and waited for them to pass.

When I finally staggered in the front door my mother came racing down the stairs to me.

"Lucy!" she nearly screamed. When she saw me limping she froze. "What happened?"

"I was at the 7-Eleven and I slipped off the curb."

"Come into the kitchen. Let's get some ice on that right away."

She sat me at the kitchen table and went to the freezer. When she came back she was holding a bag of frozen peas.

"Let me see that." She lifted my ankle onto the table to get a better look. "That must have been quite a curb," she said. I could feel she was looking at me—I didn't look back.

"I thought I wasn't supposed to have my feet on the table," I tried to joke. It wasn't very funny.

She pressed the bag down around my ankle. "Just hold that on it." She went over to grab the landline and started to press the buttons. "Your father went out looking for you."

That harmless-looking bag of peas was so cold it burned, but I didn't say anything. My mother read my mind and gave me a kitchen towel to wrap around them as she pressed the phone to her ear.

"She's home," she said into the receiver. Then she listened for a few seconds. "All right, don't race." She hung up. "Your father will be home in a few minutes."

I wished I hadn't come back.

My mother went to put a couple of pieces of bread in the toaster. I wasn't sure, but when she came back over to the table and picked up the sugar bowl, and I saw that the coffeemaker on the counter was still on, I knew what she was doing. In case you have never had it, sugar toast is a very guilty pleasure. White toast, lots of butter, a sprinkling of sugar, and a teaspoon of coffee dripped over the top. It was something my mom used to make me when I was sick—I hadn't eaten it in ages. Over the years, my mother has become much more health conscious about what she feeds us. We were even gluten free for a while last year, which was a long way from super tasty sugar toast.

As she was dripping the last bit of coffee onto the toast, my father came through the back door. He stopped when he saw my foot up on the table.

"Are you okay?" he said. The crease between his eyes was very deep. He came over to see my ankle and lifted the bag of peas. "What happened?"

"Nothing. I fell off the curb."

I was staring at my fingernails, giving them my full attention, but I could feel him look at my mother as she placed the toast in front of me.

"Keep the ice on it," he said.

I looked up for a second. His blue eyes were shimmering. He was trying very hard not to be upset, and it wasn't working. But there were so many things to be upset about at the moment, I wasn't sure exactly which one was bothering him the most.

"Why don't you go up and have a shower," my mother said to him. "Let Lucy and me talk."

My dad sighed loudly. He was still standing over me, and he reached out to touch my hair. I didn't like him touching me at that instant, but it meant he wasn't going to yell at me.

"You eat your toast with your mother, and then get on up to bed. We'll talk in the morning."

When I was on the second slice my mom came and sat down next to me. She shook her head a bit.

"What?" I asked her.

"Sometimes you remind me so much of Grandma Lucy. You're well named, my darling."

My foot was still up on the table, and I could feel my pulse throbbing in my ankle. "Tell me that story again," I said.

My mom laughed. "I haven't told you that in a long time, have I?"

My great-grandmother and namesake was Lucy Van Buskirk. She grew up in Traverse City, Michigan. Apparently she led a wild and impulsive life, especially for someone at that time.

"When she was seventeen," my mother began, "Grandma Lucy met a traveling vacuum cleaner salesman who happened to knock on the door—they did stuff like that back

then. He talked her parents into buying a vacuum that afternoon, and no one thought any more about it, until—"
And here my mother leaned forward and her voice got kind
of low. "Without her parents knowing, my grandmother
kept in touch with the salesman by writing letters. No one
even knew she got his address.

"Then, the moment she turned eighteen, against her
parents' wishes, Grandma Lucy followed after the salesman
to Denver. They had three girls together, the youngest of
which was my mother. One day she left him and took the
girls back to Michigan and raised them there on her own.
She earned money by making denim overalls and selling
them from the back of her car to the men who worked in
the cherry orchards around Traverse City."

That story always makes me feel proud to have the
name that I do.

My mother usually ends the tale there, but tonight she
went on. "But maybe the most interesting thing about it
all," she whispered, "was that Grandma Lucy may have had
a dark secret. No one is certain, but she might never have
actually been married to the salesman in the first place. Everyone just naturally assumed they were married, but no
one ever saw any record of it or went to their wedding, and
years later she let slip how glad she was that she had never
married—but then another time she denied saying such a
thing. So no one really knows."

My mom was silent for a minute.

"How come you never told me that last part before?" I asked her.

She just smiled at me and shrugged.

"How old were you when you learned that?"

"I suppose I was about your age, maybe a little older. She was an absolutely fantastic lady though, that's for certain. She was a wonderful grandmother and she adored her children until the day she died."

We sat there for a while, then my mom smiled. "So you just never know."

If she was somehow trying to compare my great-grandmother's situation to my father's, I wasn't interested.

My mother didn't have her ever-present evening glass of wine in her hand. I wondered if it was because of what I'd said to her earlier about always having a Chablis. I felt bad about the remark, but not really.

"How's that ankle doing? Let me see it." She leaned over and lifted the peas. She touched the swollen skin, which was even redder now because of the ice. "How's that feel?" she asked.

I couldn't really feel anything since it was so numb. "A little better, I think."

"If it still looks bad in the morning, we'll go in for some X-rays."

Climbing the stairs, I had one arm over my mother's shoulder and one hand pushing off the banister. My sister's door was closed; she was probably oblivious to my whole disappearing act–smashed-up ankle drama. Her music was still playing softly. My mother didn't tell her to shut it off, even though it was past lights-out.

I somehow managed to brush my teeth and get to bed. If anyone knocked on my door wanting to come in and explain himself, it didn't happen while I was awake. And I lay there in the dark for a long time.

4

THE WALLS OF THE WAITING ROOM at the X-ray place were covered in cheery posters with really uplifting and stupid sayings: *Don't Quit Five Minutes Before the Miracle*—as if you should know when that might be—and *Tomorrow's Coming, Hang On!*, etc. There were a few other posters as well, which just had puffy clouds on them. Maybe they were intended to trick us into thinking we were soaring through life, instead of sitting there on these stained couches, waiting and waiting.

I don't mean to sound cynical, because I'm not. Not usually, anyway. I'm not one of those people who are all jaded and act as if they don't care about anything and walk around as if they're exhausted by life. But those posters were killing me.

My mom had let me sleep late, so my dad was already at work by the time I hobbled into the kitchen, which was the only upside of the day so far.

A young boy and his grandmother sat across the room, waiting, too. I couldn't tell what might be wrong with them; they looked totally fine. The boy seemed to be about eight years old. He could have been this Thomas kid for all I knew.

It was my first experience with X-rays—other than the dentist, which doesn't count. The guy doing the X-rays was surprisingly young.

"Are you the doctor?" I asked him as I followed him into the small room.

He laughed. "Why, do I seem like one?" He didn't wait for me to answer. "No, I'm the technician. I'll be taking your photos." He was super gentle as he positioned my ankle in this weird way, and he had a southern accent that made everything he said sound like honey.

"This looks like a beauty," he drawled, as if he was talking about a particularly fine vegetable or something. "Must have hurt a lot."

"Not too bad." I shrugged.

That sweet-sounding technician then threw this heavy X-ray-proof blanket over my body and raced out of the room like I had a contagious disease. Maybe it was because up to that point he had been so nice, but when the door clicked behind him I never felt so alone in my entire life. Then he zapped me.

The X-rays were negative. That's exactly what the doctor in the white coat said after she looked at them for a grand total of thirty seconds: "They're negative"—very medical sounding. Of course I was glad, but frankly, part of me was disappointed. It would have served my dad right if it was broken. Instead, I was just going to have to hobble around on crutches for several days with a bad sprain.

My mom let me stay home for the rest of the day, and when my dad came in for lunch I was in the kitchen eating. He didn't have much to say to me. What was there to say? The facts were the facts. He sat down beside me and gave me his sincere look. I wasn't buying it.

"I know you're upset, Lucy," he said. "I wish I could change things, but we'll get through this. You'll see."

"It's okay," I said. I took a bite out of my sandwich. I just wanted him to go away. "These things happen."

He just looked at me when I said that. "Well, I don't know about that, Lucy, but in no way does this affect how much I love you or your sister."

Up in my room I lay on my bed, staring at the map of the world on my wall. I plan to visit all seven continents and the North Pole, and cross the seven seas. I haven't been anywhere yet—except for thirteen states, if you count driving through and airports. I've stuck pins in them all. I was just finishing the count again when my best friend Arianna texted: Where were you today?

Jumped off the roof and nearly broke my ankle

Insane

Just bored

Typical!

For some reason that remark really bothered me, especially the exclamation point.

Well, if your father had just told you that he had screwed some chick, got her pregnant, and had a kid that is running around in the world you might jump off the roof too!!

I actually considered sending that, but I didn't. I mean, how could I? I watched the cursor on my phone suck back up the words.

My mom was going to let me stay home from school again the next day since I could still hardly walk, but I couldn't stand the thought of being around the house.

Then the second I walked into school, it seemed like everyone was looking at me. The crutches felt like this giant blinking neon sign that went on and off with each plunk on the ground, blaring, *MY DAD . . . HAS ANOTHER . . . KID.*

Arianna had obviously been very busy spreading the news of my little roof jump—I caught a good deal of grief for it.

"Hey, it's Superwoman—NOT!" this computer geek named Zac said as he passed me in the hall. He thought that was very funny.

At lunch I couldn't carry my tray since I had the crutches. Ruby, this really big varsity volleyball star, was behind me in line, so she helped me out, mostly because it was the only way she was ever going to get through the line herself. The whole time she just kept shaking her head, as if she was trying to tell everyone that she didn't approve of my existence and was only stuck helping me because she was in the wrong place at the wrong time.

Eventually we made it to my usual table. Ruby almost dislocated her spine shaking her head again as she left.

"Thanks for telling everyone," I said to Arianna. I could barely squeeze my foot under the table without banging something.

"I didn't tell everyone." She shrugged. "Just some people. And it's not like no one would have known. I mean, look at you."

At that moment my crutches slipped from the side of the table where I'd leaned them and crashed to the floor. Everyone nearby looked over at the commotion.

"They wouldn't have to know I jumped off the roof," I hissed at Arianna.

"Whatever."

As if that was an explanation.

"You are way too impulsive, Willows." Arianna always called me by my last name; why, I have no idea. I think she saw somebody talk that way in a movie or somewhere. "You gotta learn to relax." She was shaking her head at me, not demonstrating a lot of sympathy. If I'd had any thoughts of sharing my real, serious news with Arianna, they evaporated right then. The rest of the day was no better. More snide remarks and stupid stares from people.

That night Arianna texted.

Hope you're not trying to fly again

What was wrong with her? I didn't even answer.

The next morning in front of my locker she came up to me. "What's with ghosting me?"

"I didn't ghost you. I just didn't answer your stupid text."

"It wasn't stupid, and I'm not the one who jumped off the roof."

I just closed my locker and hobbled to class. Clearly, whatever flair I had with people was out of sync. The next few days were no better. I started to feel like a freak, and began to give everyone a wide berth. School usually never troubled me too much, but now it was starting to stress me out. I really began to dislike going to my classes.

I also started to fall behind on these interviews I was supposed to be doing for the yearbook. A while ago I had this crazy idea to speak with various people about things that they were not very good at. For example, if someone was a great basketball player, I talked with them about what sport they were the worst at. Or if someone was very outspoken, like the president of the debating club, I asked them what they felt shy about. The yearbook advisor, Mr. Burke, thought this was actually a pretty great idea, so it became my job to interview people—twenty-four of them was the number he decided. Then they would put my interview answers on the yearbook page next to the one with those lame Senior Superlative winners—although, I suppose if you were named one, like "most likely to earn a million dollars the fastest," you wouldn't think it was so stupid. Anyway, I had to find about four people a week if I was going to have all twenty-four in time for the printing, but now I started to get behind.

The first day I didn't have my crutches, we took a field trip into New York to go to the Metropolitan Museum of Art to look at the impressionist paintings. We'd been studying that period in art history and we were supposed to find a painting we liked and sketch it.

Arianna was in my art history class, but she was getting her braces off and not at school that day. I actually didn't care all that much that she wasn't there. Frankly, I couldn't really deal with her recent attitude—I couldn't deal with anyone's attitude.

I ended up sitting next to Maxine Wagner on the bus. I

had sort of known her for years, but had never really spoken to her much or hung out with her before. She rode horses all the time and had no interest in anyone—which at this moment was fine by me.

But by the time we reached the highway, she still hadn't spoken a word, so just to be polite I said, "How are the horses treating you?"

"I quit," she said.

"Really?"

"Yup."

"Wow. Didn't you ride all the time?"

"Six days a week."

"What happened?"

She shrugged. "I grew up."

Of all the answers she could have given, I actually thought this was one of the best.

I nodded.

She nodded back. Then she broke into the biggest, warmest smile I think I have ever seen. Who knew she was capable of such a nice smile?

We had a pleasant chat about the joys of getting out of school and going into the city, but mostly we were both content to just hang out. I spent a good deal of the time gazing out the window. There's something really peaceful about seeing things zip past, knowing you don't have to deal with them—just look at them and then they're gone.

Then we disappeared into the Lincoln Tunnel. I know a lot of people dislike going into a tunnel; they find it claustrophobic or some such. But I really enjoy it. I can't help but feel that when we come out the other side, things will be different.

There was a lot of traffic in the city, like there always is, but we eventually made it through the park. At the museum, we went through security like we were getting on a plane to nowhere, then we were herded directly up the stairs and off to the left to the appointed galleries. I am not an artist. I thought since the paintings were impressionist instead of realistic they would be easier to sketch—I was wrong. I tried to do the big painting of water lilies by Monet. My sketch was a mess. It looked like a bad necklace with large teardrops hanging off it.

I didn't expect it to be any good since I'm generally so bad at artistic stuff, but I was surprised how embarrassed by it I was.

"Yours is the only one worse than mine," someone said over my shoulder.

It was Maxine. She was smiling her big open smile again. Then she held up her sketch, which was of that famous *Starry Night* painting by Van Gogh. Hers was terrible also.

After a less boring than I would have thought lecture on the "radical reactionism" of the impressionists, we had

a half hour to look at whatever else we wanted at the museum. Maxine and I went to the Egyptian section, not because I had any real interest in it, but because it was the
only place I knew. When I was little, my family used to go
to the museum occasionally and I remember I got freaked
out by the mummies. This time they just seemed really sad.
Those poor people didn't have any place to eternally rest.
When I die, I do not want my coffin sitting in some museum, not that any museum would want my coffin. I would
like to be under a tree on a hillside, or better yet, cremated
and scattered somewhere that holds deep meaning for me.
I haven't found a place like that yet, but when I do, that's
where I will want to be scattered. At sunset.

For some reason I noticed this mummy tucked over in
the corner, behind glass. It was really small; it must have
been a young person—perhaps an eight-year-old boy.

"What are you staring at?" Maxine asked.

"Nothing." Were thoughts of this Thomas kid now going
to pop up everywhere I went? That was all I needed.

The truth is that most of the mummies were fairly
small. They must have been pretty short in ancient Egypt.
I should have been born then—I would have been average
height. Of course, I probably would have been some slave
who had to carry water through the desert under the blis-
tering sun to the other slaves who were building pyramids
or the Sphinx or some such ancient ruin.

But on the off chance that I was actually royalty, my exalted status might have come in handy. Back then life was cheap, and if you were a nobleman you could get away with killing just about anyone you wanted to kill. And there were one or two people right about now that I wouldn't have minded seeing dead.

5

―――――

"YOUR MOTHER AND I THOUGHT it would be a good idea to talk about this a little more."

It was two weeks since the Thomas bomb had been dropped, and the day after my parents had gone out for a big dinner to celebrate their wedding anniversary—which I suppose qualifies as a fine example of irony.

If you had come over to our house during that two-week stretch, you wouldn't have noticed anything different from the way things had always been. My dad went off to work selling houses, my mom continued doing her layouts part-time for the magazine and chauffeuring Julie around to the various singing and dancing classes that consumed her life. Dinner was on the table each night. Everything looked the same, yet nothing was.

I had been trying to keep my head down and basically just avoid everyone, but then my father gathered us all in the living room. I couldn't remember the last time I had actually sat in that room. Everyone always passed through it on the way from the stairs to the kitchen. My dad was on the big couch next to my mother, a cup of tea in his hand. Julie and I were in the two overstuffed chairs across from them. The sun streamed in through the window over my dad's shoulder, and dust motes floated in the shaft of light. I kept my eyes on them throughout most of the talk.

"The first thing I want to say is that I love you two very, very much," my dad said. "And I love your mother very much."

My mom reached over and took his hand.

If this was the way this talk was going to go, then I was gonna puke.

"When you kids were much younger, your mother and I went to a party at a friend's home."

So this was it. He was going to tell us all the dirty details. I wondered which friends had the party. I didn't ask.

Apparently my father met a woman at said party and shortly thereafter they had a onetime fling. That was the word he used, *fling*. Seriously?

It was just the one time—or so he insisted.

He was leaning forward, his elbows resting on his knees,

the mug of tea clutched in both hands. "I didn't know there was going to be a child until months later, when I saw the woman at the train station and she was very pregnant."

"When's his birthday?" I asked. I didn't even know I was going to ask that. I had never wondered before.

"It's in September," my father said. "September 24."

"And what's his name?"

"His name is Thomas," he said calmly.

"Yeah, I know that. What's his last name?"

My parents looked at each other for a second.

"Eaves," my father said. "His name is Thomas Eaves."

The talk went on from there. At one point I looked over at my sister. I knew she was sitting beside me, but somehow I couldn't feel her there so I had to look over and make sure. She seemed very small, buried deep in the cushions of the puffy chair. She's very fair skinned, but she seemed even paler than normal. She was staring at something above my father's head. I had no idea what. A little later I thought I could just barely hear her humming "Oh, What a Beautiful Morning," one of those super old show tunes she's been singing forever. She didn't say a word the entire time.

The talk was meant to clear the air, but frankly, it was too much information and not a lot of answering the important questions, like how the hell could he do that to my mom, especially when she was at home dealing with the kids and keeping his house running? Why didn't she just take her hand out of his and punch him in the face?

I remembered once seeing a TV show about a Hollywood couple who had newborn twins. The guy had been caught cheating, and this was their first public appearance to say how their love and family was so important, and they were putting the incident behind them.

"With a new child everyone is so overtired," the starlet wife was saying, but she didn't look overtired. She looked like a movie star with perfect hair. She was sitting on the couch next to her movie star husband, just like my mom was now sitting next to my father. She went on to say that between their stellar film careers and now parenting, they just hadn't had any time for each other or for romance and that it happens more often than you'd think. It didn't mean they didn't love each other. "And from now on," she said, "we're going to have a *date night* every week just to keep things percolating." Then she turned her glimmering teeth on her A-list husband and he smiled back devilishly.

"It's just something that can happen in a long relationship," the wife concluded as the husband nodded his head.

I suppose it makes sense, but it also sounded like a bunch of excuses to me. He looked like a smug jerk, and she seemed like a total wimp.

I realized I wasn't even listening to my father anymore, and at some point I had shifted my focus from the floating dust to the oversized palm tree mug he was holding in his hand.

When I was little, about seven or eight—the same age

as that kid who lives across town—my dad used to take me to this pottery place not far from his office. It was our place, the thing that just *we* did together. You could make your own cups and bowls and various other things, or you could pick from the stuff that had been premade. Neither my dad nor I was very good at throwing pottery, but we both loved painting it.

"What are you going to do today, Dad?" I'd always ask as we walked through the glass front door.

"I think maybe today it's gonna be a mug," my dad said that particular morning he decided to paint the palm tree. He had a sly grin on his face, I remember.

We set about filling our trays with the colors we'd need. The trays held eight colors each, but that day he only squeezed out four. Usually we chatted away while we painted, and sometimes we even changed our minds about what we were painting halfway through, but that day my dad was quiet. He was really concentrating. He knew just what he wanted to do.

"Whoa! Awesome, Dad," I said when he finally let me see it. Even before it was fired it looked pretty great. "I want to go to that beach."

"Me, too," he said with a big sigh.

It took about a week after we painted the stuff for it to go through the kiln and be ready for us to pick up. As much as we loved the painting part, what I think we both

liked best, but also couldn't stand, was the anticipation of
the final product.

My dad actually got pulled over once for going through
a red light just trying to get there faster. He didn't get a
ticket because he had sold the policeman his house two
years earlier and the cop remembered him.

"Good thing he likes his house," I said after the officer
let us go. I have to admit that my dad is very good at his job.

"Sure is." My dad laughed. The truth is that the stuff
we made at that shop was usually a little disappointing.
Nothing ever turned out as good as I thought it was going
to—except for that palm tree mug. It's not that the palm
tree or the ocean was so perfect; it's just that you sort of felt
like you were at the beach when you looked at it—which
doesn't make much sense, but is really the best way I can
describe it. For some reason it exceeded all expectations,
even my mom's.

"Look at that!" she said when she saw it. "Did you really
do that, sweetheart?"

"Shocking, isn't it?" my dad said.

My mom laughed. "It is."

She usually tried to make a show of being impressed
by my stuff, even when it wasn't all that stellar, but this one
thing of my dad's caught her genuinely off guard. It was
spectacular.

And he gave it to me. Naturally, being the bighearted

person that I am, I gave him carte blanche to use it whenever he wanted. Now that I thought about it, he probably made it right around the time of the incident with the woman from the party. Disgusting. It was pretty insensitive of him to be drinking from that particular mug at that exact moment in the living room.

My mother didn't really say two words during the talk, and nothing my father said was of much interest to me. Eventually the big meeting just fizzled out.

After that, whenever I was in a room with my dad, I left as soon as I could. At first I tried to do it so he didn't notice that it was because of him.

"I've got a lot of homework," became my standard thing to say so I could leave right after dinner. Or I'd say, "Oh, I gotta find my phone," if he came into the kitchen while I was having something to drink. Not very original lines, but I didn't care.

After a little while, I stopped trying and simply walked out whenever he walked in. The sight of my dad had started to make my stomach sick.

One afternoon he caught me off guard when he came back between house showings. I hadn't expected him until dinner. I was at the kitchen table reading the newspaper. Though I generally have no interest in reading the paper, for some reason I take great pleasure in spreading it out on the kitchen table and perusing it when no one else is around.

When I started to gather it up, he stopped me.

"Lucy." He said my name with great seriousness. He was getting set to have a little heart-to-heart. You certainly had to admire his perseverance, if nothing else. He gazed down at his shoes and then looked up at me. His already big blue eyes got even bigger, and bluer, if such a thing was possible. In the past I would have said that my dad had very sincere eyes, but of course I couldn't say that anymore.

"We're going to have to talk again sooner or later," he said.

"We're not *not* talking. I've just got a term paper due." I left the room.

I didn't have any interest in anything he had to say on the subject, or any subject for that matter, even though I did actually have a lot of questions. Questions that didn't get addressed during the big talk.

Did this Thomas person have a father who was his everyday father, like a stepfather? Would it even really be a stepfather since my dad and this woman were never married or a couple? Was she married now? Was she pretty? And what was her name? Where exactly did they live? Did the woman really want no involvement between my dad and their child, as he had said? Would she change her mind? And what about his involvement with her? Was it really just that one time? Did he still like her, did he love her, or think about her? How often did he run into her at the supermarket? Was my dad ever going to go and live with them? There seemed a lot of loose strings to this situation, and it wasn't likely that I was going to get any answers, especially since I wasn't talking to the main person who would have been able to tell me everything.

And I certainly wasn't going to ask my mother. Frankly, I couldn't really deal with her either. How could she have stayed with him after what he did to her? We should have moved out when it happened, and then we'd be all set up in our new life by this point. We might not have our family, but I'd at least still have some respect for her.

Around the same time I began ducking my parents as much as possible, I wandered into Mr. Burke's office at school.

"Hey, Mr. Burke," I said from the doorway.

"Lucy, hi. I'm just running over to the yearbook meeting. We're setting the layout. Come on, we'll walk over."

"Actually, I need to talk to you about that."

"How are the interviews coming?" He was gathering a big pile of papers, not really listening.

"Yeah, you know, I actually don't think it's such a good idea anymore. I think people will think it's stupid."

He stopped sorting papers and looked at me. "What?"

"Maybe you can get someone else to do it."

"Sit down, Lucy."

I walked into his small office and he lifted a stack of papers off the chair next to his desk.

"It's a fresh and original idea, Lucy."

"Okay, but I just don't think so."

"Where's this coming from? When you came to me and presented the idea, you were so excited. It was your enthusiasm that sold us all. And now everyone is counting on you."

I stared at my hands. "I'm sorry. I just can't do it anymore." I couldn't tell him that I had only spoken to nine people. There was no way I was going to get the other fifteen interviews done in time. He was a sweet man; he didn't deserve to get ditched.

6

————

LATER THAT WEEK, one of the first almost hot days of the year arrived. All of a sudden you could really feel the end of the school year coming, thank God. Heading home, I was scuffing my feet on the sidewalk, trying to get the left and right feet to scrape evenly. For some reason it became really important for me to get them even, and the fact that I couldn't get them to scuff in the same way had begun to stress me out, so I was really glad when I heard someone call my name. It was Maxine.

"Hey," she caught up with me. "What are you doing?"

"I'm trying to skim the ground the same on each foot,

but I can't quite do it; my left keeps scraping a little bit more than my right."

"Why are you doing that?"

"I don't know."

She tried it for a few steps, then basically lost interest. "Want to head over to my house?"

It turned out that Maxine lived just a few blocks past my house, in the direction that I never go, away from town and school. It was like going to a totally new place on the map, which felt refreshing.

Her house was a yellow stucco structure with dark beams that cut through it at diagonals; it didn't look like any other house on the block. Apparently her parents were never home after school, so we could just hang out. I'm not quite sure where Maxine had gotten her reputation for not liking anyone, but it was proving to be false—she was surprisingly easy to be with. Plus, she was the only person I knew other than me who wasn't into staring at her phone all day long. The only thing that she really liked to do was post random photos occasionally—just let them speak for themselves, let people read whatever meaning they wanted into them.

"Do you miss your horse riding?" I asked her when we were taking pictures of our hands.

"I'm kind of surprised," she said, and snapped a super tight photo of the lines in her palm. "But I don't miss it at all. I hardly even think about it. It's like there was that life, now there's this life. You know what I mean?"

"Yeah," I said. I wanted to tell her that I knew exactly what she meant. I hadn't considered mentioning Thomas to anyone since Arianna betrayed me with her callousness, but I almost said something there in Maxine's room.

"It's kind of a relief," she said, and started bending the tip of her finger back.

I was glad that at least *her* new life was better.

"Does the tip of your finger do this?" She was bending it back till it looked like it hurt.

"Ow! No. Gross. You must be double-jointed or something."

Later, we were in the kitchen, on the stools at the counter. We were drinking 7 Ups when this kid walked in. His hair was long, and if it hadn't swooped off to the right just below his eyebrows, it would have gone down past his nose. He was wearing a T-shirt and his arms were really skinny and he looked at the ground when he walked, like he had lost something important and was searching carefully for it. He didn't say anything. He just went to the fridge and stuck his head in it for a long time.

"Where's the 7 Up?" he said when he emerged.

"We drank the last two," Maxine said.

He didn't say anything else; he just turned without looking at me even once and left. I heard him walking up the stairs.

"My brother," Maxine said.

"I didn't know you had a brother," I said.

As we were going back up to Maxine's room, he was coming out of the bathroom, wiping his hands on his pants.

"I'm Lucy," I said as he passed.

"Simon," he mumbled. He brushed up against the wall and hunched his shoulders as he went. His hair fell into his face. He was very tall. "How's it going?"

"It's going good," I told him. I had this crazy urge to reach up and push his swooping bangs away from his eyes, but he had already gone into his room. The door shut before I finished my sentence.

"What grade is your brother in?" I asked Maxine when I walked back into her room. She lay down on her bed, with her head dangling off the side, and tried to drink her 7 Up upside down.

"He's a junior."

"But he doesn't go to our school?" I half asked, half said. I was being a bit cagey with my questions. I wasn't exactly sure why—maybe I was distracted by his wavy hair.

"No, he goes to Meadowlark. It's a special school for people with learning issues."

"What's his issue?"

Apparently Simon had to spend a lot of time learning to organize information and compose research papers and whatnot. "My parents won't medicate him, so he has to learn how to harness his distractions."

"That's cool," I said. The way Maxine put it, it didn't sound that serious to me.

Then the next time I was at Maxine's, I was just looking out her bedroom window when I saw Simon in the backyard. He was by the edge of the garage. He kept poking his head out of sight around the corner looking for something. Maxine distracted me by showing off this new shirt she had bought, but when she went to the bathroom I looked out the window again.

Maybe I was looking for Simon, or maybe I was just looking—I'm not one hundred percent sure. In any event, Simon was still doing his searching-for-something-around-the-corner-of-the-garage act, so I decided to go out and see what was going on.

"Get out of here," he said when he saw me coming across the backyard. I couldn't tell if he meant it or not, but he was smiling so I decided to ignore his words and just kept walking until I was right next to him. I looked around the corner of the garage. There was nothing but a big pile of old leaves, grass clippings, and a stack of wood, with a few rakes and shovels leaning up against the garage.

"What are you looking for?" I asked him.

"Nothing." He opened the palm of his hand. In it was a small metal pipe, with a faint wisp of smoke coming out of the tiny bowl.

I thought I had smelled something as I was walking over. It's not like I didn't smell pot all the time. In the mornings, you couldn't walk past the woods a block from school and not get knocked over by the clouds wafting out of there. But the potheads I knew all hung out together.

"Want a hit?" Simon asked.

I shrugged. "Sure."

"Stick your head around the corner," he told me.

He hadn't been looking for anything at all. He was actually poking his head around the corner of the garage to smoke. Then, after exhaling, he'd go back to standing normally and make sure one of his parents' cars wasn't coming up the driveway.

He handed me the pipe. I leaned over and put it up to my mouth; it was still wet from his lips. He lit a match and held it over the bowl. I sucked in really hard and instantly began coughing my lungs out. I almost dropped the pipe. He started laughing, then slapped my back a few times. "Are you okay?"

"It's been a while," I said, when I finally stopped coughing.

"Yeah," Simon said. He pulled his hand away, but I could still feel the spot where it had been.

We then traded the pipe back and forth a few times. I took a couple of smaller hits and didn't cough as much.

When we were walking back toward the house he said, "Don't worry, you don't get high the first time."

Then the next time I saw Simon I didn't actually see him at all. I was walking past his room on my way upstairs from the kitchen. I had gone down to get some sodas for Maxine and me, and his door was open a few inches. I'd swear it had been closed when I walked past on the way down.

"How's it going?" I heard from inside the room.

I stopped in the hall and backed up a few feet, so I was standing right outside the door. I couldn't see in, but I knew he was there.

"I'm okay," I said. "How you doing?"

"I'm cool," he said.

I was just hanging there in limbo-land.

"How was school?" I sounded like my parents.

"Fine," he said. "Almost done, thank God."

"Yeah, I know what you mean," I said.

I stood there for a minute. "You want a Coke?" I had two in my hands, one for me and one for Maxine.

"No, I'm good."

For the life of me, I couldn't think of anything else to say.

"Okay, well, good to see you," I said, although of course I hadn't seen him at all.

"You, too," Simon said.

When I went back into Maxine's room she was sending out a picture of her betta fish.

"Is your brother kind of weird sometimes?" I asked her.

"Not really." She shrugged. "Why?"

7

APPARENTLY, ROMEO AND JULIET SPOKE only 117 words to each other before they kissed for the first time. I know this useless bit of information because last year, when my ninth-grade English class read the play, Heather Simton—who some of my peers liked to call Heather *Simple*ton—counted.

"It just seemed way too fast to be believable," she said.

"That's because she was a slut," Rick Vemond, one of the most popular kids in my grade—and one of its most dangerous assholes—blurted out from the last row. How he was so popular I could not understand. No, that's not really true, I knew why. He was very handsome, with incredibly sexy dirty blond hair. And his girlfriend was Deidre

Messier, a tall willowy figure. If you took away those two things, he would have lost a great deal of his appeal. Which also happened when he spoke.

"Thank you very much, Mr. Vemond. An insightful observation, as always," our English teacher, Mr. Schneider, said. "Actually, at this point in the text, act 1, scene 5, after delivering the backstory of the families and setting the stage for things to come, the plot needs to be propelled forward. And more important, the kiss gives us an indication of the urgency of their love."

Mr. Schneider seemed to be the last person on earth to understand love's urgency. He was bald and round—not that chubby people with no hair can't be in love. It's just that everything he did, he did so slowly that *urgency* was simply not a word I would have ever used in relation to him. But I suppose you never know what love's arrow will do to you—or when it will strike.

For example, the first time Simon kissed me we were out by the garage, smoking weed. Not quite as romantic as some fancy Elizabethan costume ball, but I'm no Juliet, and frankly, Simon does not have Romeo's way with words.

Simon was doing more smoking than I was. I wasn't really doing any. The stuff mostly just made me feel spacey, and I couldn't seem to smoke without coughing. I wasn't even sure how much Simon liked it, either. I suppose the best part about the whole thing was the way Simon looked at me while he held his breath after he took a hit. He would end up bugging his eyes out, or puffing up his cheeks, whatever, just to make me laugh. Which he always did.

"Come back here," he said, and walked around the corner of the garage, beside the pile of old grass clippings. There wasn't much room between the pile and the pricker bushes that grew between the trees.

"What?" I said as I stepped toward the pile, keeping my eye on the thorns. All my life I always seem to get caught in those things, and I didn't want it to happen there with him. When I looked up from the thorns, he was standing really close and leaning down toward me. It was an odd sensation, exacerbated by the fact of my slightly less than average stature, which made him seem even taller. He looked like some kind of bird, a stork or something, bending toward me. I didn't know what was happening and then he was kissing me. He pushed his tongue against my mouth. I kind of pulled away because it surprised me. But obviously I knew what to do, and so after a second I opened my mouth.

"You have to use your tongue," he said.

"I am," I told him. I admit, I was a bit defensive, but I didn't like being told how to kiss. Granted, I didn't have a whole ton of experience at it—but still, a girl likes to find her own way.

I think I had been waiting for Simon to kiss me from that first time I saw him and wanted to push his hair back, so I was glad it was finally game on. I grabbed his shirt, pulled him toward me, and went for it. I may have been a bit overeager because I think I made him gag a little, but things settled down after that and it was actually pretty fun in that gross kind of way.

I will confess now that I was very late to the whole sex thing. I am slightly embarrassed to admit this, but it's simply a fact—after fifteen and a half years of life, this was my first real kiss. I had a few chances to make out before, most notably with this good-looking kid named Todd Scully after the fall choir concert, but up close he had bad breath, so I declined. There were a few other opportunities as well, but they never presented themselves in a way that I felt good about. Then, of course, when you don't do something that you want to do—especially if everyone else is constantly doing it—it becomes even more difficult to break through. But smooching Simon helped me to see the reasons behind why I never did it before. It was much easier to admit that in the past I had simply been afraid—which for someone like me, who does not like to show that particular emotion, had been a challenge. But now, with our faces mashed firmly together, I was in the club. All in all, this was perhaps one of the three most exciting and pleasurable things that had ever happened to me.

After that, whenever I would go over to Maxine's and Simon was there, Maxine and I would hang out for a while, and then I would make some kind of excuse and go to the bathroom or down to the kitchen to get a Coke, and on the way back, Simon's door would be open and I'd pop in and say hello. Usually he was sitting on the futon mattress that was bent up like a couch on the floor. He was often messing with his phone. I'd go sit next to him on the futon and we'd just start kissing. Usually we'd say a few things first, such as, "How's it going?" or something clever like that—generally it was way less than 117 words. Then we'd begin kissing. But we didn't always speak first. Sometimes I just went over to the couch and sat down next to him. After a few minutes I'd head back to Maxine's room— she never asked where I'd been.

I didn't think she even knew about our extracurricular activity, and then one day I walked back into her room and she was reading horoscopes from one of those ridiculous teen magazines.

"What's your sign?" she said after I flopped on the bed beside her.

"Sagittarius."

She was quiet for a bit while she read.

"Says here you're going on a journey soon, and being a Sag"—her voice changed to sound all moody and mysterious—"let your natural inquisitiveness be your guide." She was silent again while she read some more. When she spoke again she was just herself. "Oh, and romance is peaking around the eighteenth of the month. So I guess you'll want to make sure Simon is around and doesn't get detention or anything like that."

I'm not a big blusher, but I could feel my cheeks getting red.

"It's cool," Maxine said. "He's good people. But make sure that it's just kissing." Then she smiled that big open smile of hers.

"What's September 24?" I asked her.

"Um, let's see . . ." She consulted her magazine. "Ah, Libra. The scales of justice."

Some justice, I thought.

"Shall I read on?" Maxine asked.

"No, doesn't matter," I lied to her.

At home things were the same. Dinner at six thirty, clean the kitchen, avoid the parents. They acted like they always had, as if there wasn't some eight-year-old Libra child who lived somewhere in town who was my dad's kid. Then one day I swear I saw him—Thomas.

The day after school let out for the summer, I was at the mall with Maxine. I'd hardly noticed school the last few weeks of class. It didn't seem to matter; I basically did just the same in my finals as I had all semester. I don't know what that says about how much attention school usually gets from me, but it was done and now I was free. At least my body was free; my mind was still the prisoner of this eight-year-old I had never met.

Simon wasn't with us at the mall. He never went out with us. Maxine and I were eating hot pretzels from Auntie Molly's, sitting on a bench outside the Sunglass Hut, when this skinny kid with short brown hair, carrying what was obviously a new baseball glove, went zipping past. There was no way to tell for sure, but he sort of looked like my dad. I have only ever seen one picture of my dad as a little kid—he was sitting on a split-rail fence with a really sweet smile on his face. My dad has always had a lovely smile—he's lucky. But it was more the feeling I got when I saw the kid in the mall than the way he looked. A chill went down my spine. I got up to follow him.

"Where are you going?" Maxine said. She jumped up and chased after me.

I didn't say anything as I shadowed the boy. It was pretty crowded, but it was fairly easy to keep up with him. It was odd that an eight-year-old was alone in the mall, but you could tell by the way he walked that he knew where he was going. He glided up the escalator. We followed.

"What are we doing?" Maxine asked.

I didn't answer, not only because I didn't know what to say, but because I couldn't really talk. There was a large lump in my throat. When the boy got off the escalator, he swung back and went into a day spa called Dashing Diva. He went to a woman who was getting her nails done and showed her the mitt. She could have been his mother; she was about the right age. She was pretty; she had long, straw-colored hair. She didn't seem to be wearing any makeup, so it seemed kind of odd that she was getting her nails done. I just stood looking at them through the glass. Maxine was beside me. She wasn't talking anymore. All of a sudden a guy joined them; maybe he was the husband. He arrived as

if he'd been running to catch up. He tussled the boy's hair.
The boy didn't seem to notice; he just continued to show
the woman the glove. When they looked out toward the
front of the shop, I bolted.

Then, a few weeks later, I thought I saw Thomas again.
Same feeling up my spine, same lump in my throat, only
this time it was a different kid. He was kind of chubby, but
with blond hair—he even had glasses. I was walking down
Elm Street with my mother, on our way back from picking
up flowers for some charity event thing she was cohosting.
The boy was going the other way, right past us, beside an
older boy. It had never occurred to me that Thomas could
have brothers or sisters. I stopped in my tracks.

"Come on, sweetheart," my mother said. "We're late,
we've got to get home."

I didn't know what to do. I couldn't just start going up
to random kids and asking them who their dad was.

And that was another thing: I didn't know if this
Thomas person knew that my dad was his dad. It was one
more of the many things my parents forgot to talk about
when they sat us down to tell us everything. What the hell
did the kid know, or think? A lot of people were affected by
this onetime fling.

When we got back to the house, I told my mom I was
going over to Maxine's.

"How come she never comes over here?" I had been
wondering when she would finally ask this.

"She will. Can I go?"

My mom was already deep into her flower arrangements for the charity event that night. I think she was glad to see me leave.

Part of the pleasure of going to Maxine's house was the walk over. Since it was away from town and on a side street, traffic was much lighter, and I never passed anyone I knew on the way. I was anyone I wanted to be.

One block had a bunch of old trees that formed a canopy over the road, and as I came out of the tunnel of leaves, the sun was shining. I slowed way down and moved as little as I could without actually stopping. I was watching my shadow hardly move. It was a childish game, but it was also quite peaceful. When I sped up again, it was disappointing in a way, and at the same time, I felt really powerful. If there had been any ants crawling across the sidewalk, I might have held my shoe over them for an instant before I let them live. I am not an ant crusher.

I cut across Maxine's front yard and went up the two steps of her stoop. Simon answered the door. He was wearing a black T-shirt that said *The Ramones* on the front. It was too small for him. His long arms stuck out like beanpoles. I looked down and his feet were bare. He had exceedingly, elegantly long and tapering toes. Wow.

"Maxine's not here," he said.

"Oh," I said. "Where'd she go?"

"She's at the store with my mother."

I kind of stood there on the stoop for a minute. I wasn't sure what to do. I mean, I had come over to see Maxine, right? I had *always* come to see Maxine. That I ended up kissing Simon for a little while most times was purely a bonus.

"You can come in if you want," Simon said.

I shrugged. "All right."

He turned and walked away, leaving me there. I watched him walk up the stairs as I closed the door. He moved like his joints were connected by rubber bands, everything all loose and swinging. It was a cool walk. Very Simon.

I didn't know exactly what to do, so I followed him. By the time I got upstairs, he was sitting in his usual position on the futon. He was picking his nails the way he sometimes did. The window was open a few inches. There was a nice breeze coming in. I'd never noticed before that his room had always felt kind of stuffy, but not on this day. I sat down next to him in my normal spot. Then Simon smiled at me—which felt very nice. Whereas Maxine had a big open smile, Simon had the sweetest, goofiest grin. There were two fine faces for smiling in that family, that's for sure.

"You know, your sister didn't tell me about you," I said.

"Didn't tell you *what* about me?"

"That you existed. I didn't know she had a brother until you walked into the kitchen that day."

"And you're telling me this now because . . . ?"

"Um, I don't know. Maybe 'cause we're alone."

"Well, it's not surprising she didn't tell you. She doesn't really notice anyone but herself."

"That's not very nice. She likes you."

"I like her too," he said. "She's my sister. I love her. I wasn't being mean—it's just true. She's kind of wrapped up in her own thing."

"Well." I shrugged. "Isn't everybody?"

Simon gave me one of his soulful gazes. "True that," he said. Then he leaned in to kiss me.

I guess he could tell I had other things on my mind, because he stopped after a bit.

"You okay?" He leaned back in order to have a good Simon look at me.

"I have a brother, too," I said.

"Oh, yeah?" Simon looked at me. "Older or younger?"

"He's eight."

Simon nodded.

"I also have a sister who's thirteen," I said.

It was no big deal to him. Why should it be? Lots of people have sisters and brothers.

I got up and went to the window. It could have used some curtains. Poor guy—how did he sleep in the morning with no blinds or shade? There were tons of fingerprints on the glass.

"Your window's open," I said.

"Yeah, it's a nice day."

He came over and stood next to me to look out. He

pressed his fingers up against the glass and leaned his nose close to it, as if he was looking through a store window at Christmastime.

Now I knew how all the fingerprints had gotten there. We were both looking out, up into the blue sky. There were very few clouds on the horizon.

"Ever wish you could just fly away?" I asked him.

"All the time," Simon said.

8

IT OCCURRED TO ME that perhaps I was losing my mind. I couldn't go around thinking every eight-year-old I saw was Thomas. It had to stop. I definitely did not want to be going crazy. That's all I needed, on top of everything else. But what could I do about it?

I walked into my sister's room. She was listening to her old musicals, per usual. Some twangy woman was singing

> *Anything you can do,*
> *I can do better.*
> *I can do anything*
> *Better than you.*

The one thing that gets Julie truly excited is the musicals that she acts in at camp during the summer. One was about to start up soon. She likes the school plays, too, but those aren't musicals; they're just regular talking plays. You have to be in high school to be in the school musicals. So she has to wait.

Personally I'm just not into getting up in front of people and dancing around and pretending to be a poor orphan with fake smudges on my cheeks or an old lady with a bad wig and a cane. But my sister loves it.

I hadn't seen much of Julie lately. It sounds stupid to say since we ate breakfast and dinner together pretty much every day, but it was like she had just sort of become invisible around the house, even when she was in the same room.

"What are you doing?" I asked her as I walked in.

"Listening to music," she said.

She could have at least turned it down when I started talking.

Suddenly some guy started singing too, going back and forth with the woman; they were arguing about who was better at everything.

"It's creepy about this Thomas kid, isn't it?" I said to Julie when the song was just about done.

"Who?"

I thought she was joking. "Uh . . . Dad's other kid, Thomas."

"Oh." She nodded. Her hair fell in front of her face.

"Yeah." It was as if I had reminded her of an old pair of skinny jeans she used to wear, or some other ancient memory that didn't matter all that much.

"I love this song!" Julie said as the next tune fired up. The singer was going on about how folks were dumb where she came from, but that didn't matter; they got by just "doing what comes naturally." What was the matter with everyone? Was I really the only person even slightly bothered by this Thomas catastrophe?

I left Lucy and her singing farmers and walked down into the kitchen. I was standing at the sink, filling a glass, when my dad came through the back door.

"Ah, right. I meant to pick up some bottled water," he said. "You know, we used to drink from the tap all the time. When I was your age, if you told me that one day people would pay a good amount of money just to have water in a bottle, I would have said you were nuts."

"Times change." I shrugged.

My dad turned on the stove under the teakettle, and then opened the cabinet and grabbed the palm tree mug and tossed a teabag in it. How many times in my life had I seen him do this exact same thing? He shook his head. "I sound like my father," he said. "Sorry."

I could tell my dad was making an effort to reach out to me, especially since he was talking about his father. He didn't mention him that often. They never got along.

"My father never really liked me very much," I once

heard my dad say. It seemed a very weird thing to think—how could a father not like his kid? Apparently, his father also had a particularly bad temper.

The one and only time that I had met my grandfather, he had seemed quite nice, and not angry at all. He only had teeth in the left side of his mouth, but that didn't stop him from having a huge appetite, even though he was skinny. He loved to eat. And he especially loved ice cream—how bad could he be?

He lived up in Maine. We finally visited him a couple of summers ago, after my sister and I saw a picture of him and badgered my father about how come we'd never met him.

My mother jumped all over that. I heard her talk to my dad about it several more times when they thought no one was around. My dad always answered her with things like, "Yeah, we'll go up sometime," but you could tell he didn't mean it. She wouldn't let it go. Finally, we piled into the car.

My dad said he would only stay at my grandfather's house for one night, so we stopped at an inn in New Hampshire on the way. After two days at this inn, kayaking and goofing around, we headed to Maine. It was a lot nicer than my dad had led us to believe. His father had moved to this small town by the ocean a long, long time ago, when he and his wife got divorced. My grandmother died a few years after that—I never met her. My grandfather married a woman from Germany, and they lived in a big house on a hill a few blocks away from a small harbor. Supposedly a sea captain had lived in it back in Ye Olde Days.

They were waiting for us in the driveway when we arrived. My grandfather was kind of nervous, you could tell. But his wife, Angela, brought us all into the kitchen to make fruit smoothies together and everyone settled down.

Meanwhile, out in the living room, my dad was staring at something. "I haven't seen this table in twenty years," he said. Then he said the same thing about a bookcase and a picture on the wall. He walked around the house just shaking his head.

After dinner my grandfather pushed his chair back from the table and folded his hands over his stomach.

"I know a place that has the best ice cream in the world. Who's in?"

"Me," my sister shrieked. She had never really been that into ice cream as far as I knew, but she sure was on this night. It had started raining really hard and my dad said he'd drive, but my grandfather wanted us to drive his car, so my dad got behind the wheel. Only one headlight worked and it was really difficult to see since there were no street-lights and it was pouring.

After a while my grandfather said, "You must have passed it."

My dad sighed and started to make a U-turn when my sister saw a big ice cream cone sign down the road. It wasn't lit up or anything, so how she saw it in the rain and dark I will never know.

The place had a tall, pointy roof like a Swiss chalet. There was nowhere to go and eat inside, and the parking lot was empty. You ordered through one window and picked up from another. The roof ended right above where you stood to order, and there were no gutters, so water was cascading down. We huddled close to the building but started to get soaked anyway, so we all raced back to the car—except for my dad, who stood getting drenched as he ordered for everyone.

Once we all had our ice cream, we started back. My grandfather was sitting up front next to my father. He was very quiet at this point, eating his ice cream, which, I have to say, was very good. It was soft serve. It was maybe not the best in the world, but still very good. I had a vanilla cone with chocolate sprinkles, my sister had a vanilla-chocolate combo with rainbow sprinkles, and my grandfather was eating a large hot-fudge sundae. I had certainly never seen such an old person eat a hot-fudge sundae before, especially one that big. I don't think my dad had, either, because he kept looking over at his father, watching him eat.

"What is it, Dad?" I asked him when he wouldn't stop looking over at his father.

My dad just shook his head—he was doing a lot of shaking his head on this trip. "I had no idea you liked ice cream," he said to his father.

"More than anything in the world," my grandfather said. Chocolate sauce was dripping down his chin and he swallowed the giant final gulp of his hot-fudge sundae. My dad handed him a napkin. My grandfather wiped his chin, but he must have missed a spot because my dad handed him another.

"Your chin," he said.

"A two-napkin sundae—must have been a good one," my grandfather said.

That was two summers ago. My dad never talked about going up to Maine again, except whenever Julie or I would ask if we could go, and he would mumble something like, "We'll go back up sometime," which was obviously his code for "We're never going back there again."

The idea that he had only taken us up to meet my grandfather once now seemed totally insane to me—really selfish. Because of some stupid feud, or whatever it was, I had been deprived of my grandfather.

The kettle on the stove started to shriek but before my father could reach for it to make his tea, my arm swept out and in one lightning-fast move I knocked that palm tree mug off the counter and onto the ground, where it shattered into a million pieces.

"Lucy!" my father yelled.

I froze where I was.

My father didn't say anything else. He just slowly turned to the counter to get some paper towels. He crouched down and started picking up the pieces.

"Move your foot please, Lucy," he said.

That snapped me out of my trance. I bolted up to my room. My father didn't call after me. He should have. He should have done something.

The door slammed behind me and I grabbed for my phone. Simon had given me his number after one of our make-out sessions and we had texted a few times, but this was our first call.

He had told me that he wasn't that into talking on the phone, and right from the start it was pretty easy to see why. He wasn't very good at it. He just kind of mumbled answers to my questions and didn't ask me much of anything. Until I told him about what had just happened in the kitchen and the whole history of the mug.

"Why'd you do that?"

"I don't know. I just got mad at him for some reason."

I left out the mysterious little brother part of the story.

He was silent for a long moment. "Well," he said eventually, "now he can't use it anymore." It was a fairly obvious thing to say.

"Yeah," I said.

Then he stated another maybe less obvious fact: "And now you don't have it either." It wasn't so much what he said, but the way his voice seemed to contain all the sadness I felt that made me glad I had called.

I started to cry a bit but was careful not to sniffle or anything, and we didn't speak for a while.

"Are you picking your nails?" I asked him.

"No."

I knew he was lying.

"Yes," he said.

Then it was quiet again. I didn't mind not talking so much now. The silence between us went up into outer space, riding on those electromagnetic waves to the satellites in their geosynchronous orbits thousands of miles above our lonely planet, then banged around the heavens for a few milliseconds before being projected back down to Earth and into our ears a few blocks from each other. I pressed the phone closer.

9
___

FINDING THOMAS'S ADDRESS was fairly simple. It took
about five minutes on the computer to figure out that there
were only three people with the last name of Eaves living
in our town. What was weird was that it had taken me so
long to think to do it. I have no excuse that it was only now
coming into my head.

I rode my bike to the first house on the list, which was
near Tamaques Park, where we skate sometimes in the win-
ter if it's cold enough and the ice gets thick enough so you
won't crash through and drown or die of hypothermia or
various other tragic consequences of unvarnished nature.

I waited for nearly two hours outside a small, gray,

one-story house that needed a new paint job. About ten minutes before I was going to have to leave to get home for dinner, a blue car with a big dent on the right passenger side rolled down the street and turned into the driveway. An old guy who was bent kind of sideways emerged from the car and shuffled toward the door.

"Excuse me," I called out. The old man turned and looked toward me as if no one had ever stopped him on his front lawn before. He seemed totally confused by what was happening—not scared or anything, just completely surprised anyone would call out to him like I had. I was standing next to my bike in the gutter. Since I was pretty positive this was the wrong place, it was easy to use the speech I'd prepared. I stepped toward him.

"I'm selling subscriptions for *National Geographic Kids* magazine and I wonder if you might like to purchase one for the child in your home." I smiled. I thought the smile was a nice touch.

"There are no kids here, young lady," he said, and he sort of smiled back at me. It was one of those old-person smiles when their face doesn't fully cooperate anymore. "My kids are all grown up and have kids older than you." He actually had a very nice, gentle voice, which, given the way that he had looked at me at first, surprised me.

"Oh well," I chirped, keeping up the happy saleswoman act. "That's a shame. I must be on my way to look for another home with children." I hopped on my bike.

"There are three kids next door." The old man pointed to the house next to his. There was a soccer ball in the front yard sitting by the bushes, in case I needed proof.

"I'm afraid they're not on my list," I shouted over my shoulder as I started to pedal away. Only after I was half-way down the block did it occur to me that it was a good thing he didn't have children, since I didn't have a magazine or clipboard or anything else to make it look like I was a genuine salesperson.

The next afternoon I decided to flip a coin about which house on the list to go to next. It was an odd thing to do, given that I had never flipped a coin to decide anything in my life. But I pulled out a quarter, rested it between my bent thumb and forefinger, and sent it up into the air with a flick of my digit. I decided to let it land on the ground instead of catching it—I didn't want to interfere in any way with what the fates decided. It was tails, so I skipped the second address and went right to number three on the list: 28 Beachwood Place, unit 2B. The unit 2B part was interesting, since there were very few apartment buildings in my town. In fact, I knew no one who lived in an apartment building. The idea of it began to fascinate me. What must it be like to hear your neighbors through the walls, or meet them in the hallway, or open those tiny metal mailboxes by the front door of the building? What happened when you got a large package?

I began to get a very clear image of what the place

looked like. But, of course—and by this point I should
have known—like all my other premonitions regarding
this Thomas person, the image in my mind of his place
was completely incorrect.

In reality, the building was part of a complex of three
rather small, two-story buildings with a mini–parking lot
next to each. From across the street, it looked like there
were six buzzers on the front door of number 28. The
whole street looked kind of new. It was a really short block
that dead-ended in a big circle to turn around in when you
came down the street by accident, which was the only reason you would come down it unless you lived in one of
these three small apartment buildings or if you were looking for an eight-year-old boy who happened to be related
to you.

Across the street, there were no houses, only a small
park with some big trees. What made it a park instead of
just a field were the three benches spread out at even inter-
vals. The one I sat on was directly across from number 28.

Another startling fact about this address was that it was
exactly six blocks from my own home. Six blocks, and I
had never been down this street. I had never even known
it existed.

I began to get that feeling between my shoulder blades,
the one that makes me so uncomfortable, so I figured I was
probably in the right spot. I didn't have to wait long for
proof. The second car to turn down the block made a right

into the small parking lot across the street from me. It was a dark green SUV. Not one of those huge, horrible ones; it was actually pretty cute. A sandy-haired woman who looked a little younger than my mom got out of the driver's seat. Her face was pleasant enough from where I sat, not a beauty or anything, just rather normal. My mother was much prettier. The woman opened the back door and a boy, about eight years old, popped out. There was no lightning bolt or even a shiver down my spine like the other times when I thought I saw him; it was just a kid with dark wavy hair. He was kind of skinny, but not too skinny. He wore blue jeans and a red T-shirt and sneakers. Typical boy's clothes, no big deal. I couldn't hear every word, since I was in the park across the street, but you could tell he was in the middle of talking about some TV show or video game or something. His mother was listening, in that parent way of not really listening but occasionally going "uh-huh" and "oh" and things like that. They walked toward the building, she got out her keys, and they went in. The door closed behind them.

I didn't know what to do next. There was nothing *to* do. I didn't feel like going home, so I just sat there. A bird, a sparrow I think, landed on the grass not too far away and started pecking at stuff that only birds can see. Then another one of the same kind of bird landed nearby and started doing the same. You could tell they were together, even though they didn't even look at each other. I never really spent a lot of time watching birds, but it was actually fascinating seeing them snap their little beaks down into the grass and then yank their heads back up. They'd take a few jerky steps and do it again. They seemed content. It seemed like a good life.

Just then the front door of number 28 opened again and the kid I'd seen came out with a skateboard. He dropped it on the sidewalk with a bang and hopped on it. With his right foot, he pushed off and went zipping down the street toward the turnaround. He went all the way around and then started to come back up the sidewalk on my side. It was odd that there was a sidewalk on my side of the street since there were no houses, but maybe they had been planning to build them on both sides and just ran out of money and so they stuck in a few benches and decided to call it a park. In any event, the kid came up the block in my direction. Pushing off and then coasting, pushing off, then coasting. It looked like he was enjoying himself well enough. He didn't notice me as he passed. When he got to the end of the street, where it ran into Prospect Avenue, which was a much busier road, he turned around and came back.

"Hey," I shouted as he was passing. I had no intention of doing this—it just came out.

He looked up, startled, and stumbled off his skateboard. He put his foot on it to keep it from rolling away.

"Oh," he said. "Hi."

"What's your name?" I asked him.

"Thomas," he said. "What's yours?"

"My name is Lucy," I told him. That name didn't seem to mean anything to him, so I stood up, got on my bike, and rode the six blocks home.

10

IT WAS A FAIRLY HOT SUMMER. The sprinkler was on a
lot in the front yard. Some days, before I walked over to
Maxine and Simon's house, I would just stroll slowly right
through it. I'd always be dry by the time I got to their place.
If I wasn't heading over there, I generally hung out in my
room. It's not like I had a whole host of better choices. The
last people I wanted to see were my father and, to a lesser
degree, my mother. Julie had basically vanished from the
face of the earth. I couldn't remember the last time I heard
her say two words.

One day I was thoroughly bored, so for no reason at all,
I started to shift some of my furniture around by shoving

the dresser to the other side of the room beside the desk, which then had to be moved to where the dresser used to be so that things wouldn't be too off balance. It looked kind of strange since the mirror that used to be over the dresser was now above the desk, but since I couldn't get the nail out of the wall to move it, I just left it there.

I had a bookcase beside the desk. Once I started going through it I realized that no one must have cleared off the shelves since I was little. There were books dating back to elementary school. There was even a cardboard book about the letters of the alphabet falling from a coconut tree. I don't think I had ever read it; it must have been Julie's and somehow, as with many things, her junk ended up cluttering my world. There was another book I hadn't thought of in years, but one my mom and dad used to read to me a lot. It was a large book, very Japanese, with great paintings inside, about an old farmer. I kept that one, but brought the alphabet book and a couple dozen others down to the living room and dumped them on the bookshelf there.

Since I was in the cleaning-out mood I kept going. The next thing to go was the picture of flowers in a vase above the bed. I probably should have thrown it out, but I don't believe in destroying art, no matter how lame it might be, so I put it in the garage.

I cleaned out my desk, which looked neat on top but was a jumble of papers and junk inside the drawer. For some reason there were all these paper clips scattered around inside. Does anyone even use paper clips anymore? I will bet you that the next generation of kids will not even know what a paper clip is. Out they went.

Next I attacked my dresser and closet. I got a big green garbage bag, the kind my dad uses to throw junk in when he cleans the yard. Then I decided to get rid of every piece of clothing I owned that had any brown in it. That added up to quite a lot of clothes. At first I put aside things that I liked a lot, but that pile started to get pretty big, so in one move I chucked it all in together. When I was done, the bag was bulging.

I was going to ask my mother to take it to the Goodwill place, but I didn't want her or my father involved in my life. Then I remembered this dumpster-type clothing donation bin in the corner of the parking lot at the train station. I hoisted the bag up on my shoulder and marched out the front door. I felt a bit like Santa Claus walking down the street, but the bag got pretty heavy pretty fast, and soon I was stopping every twenty feet to rest. By the time I got the five blocks to the train station downtown, my shoulders and arms were killing me. The big bin had a door with a hinge on it and a sign indicating how to deposit the clothes inside. The door looked heavy, but it just slid open with no effort at all. I hoisted the clothes one last time and dumped everything in. I could hear them hit the bottom of the bin. Either someone had just collected all the donations, or no one in my town was helping the poor. By that time, I was all sweaty. I reached into my pocket to see if I had enough money for a smoothie and found a few dollars and a bunch of coins.

Instead of going across the street to Juice Dream, I walked up to the train station. I went right through the waiting room—it had that musty train station smell—and out to the platform. There were two sets of tracks—one that took trains into the city, and another that carried them farther into the wilds of Jersey. I looked up and down in each direction. Off to my right, I thought I could see a train coming from very far away. No one was around, so I hopped down onto the stones and took a coin from my pocket, a penny, and I laid it on the nearest track. I started to step away and then I grabbed another coin from my pocket, a dime. The train was getting closer and I put the dime down next to the penny. I went to climb back up onto the platform. It was higher than I thought and I got scared for a second, but my fear gave me strength and up I went.

This trick with the coins was something that my dad had taught me when I was little. We did it a few times, till my mother got wind of it. You've never heard anyone so angry in your life.

"Are you out of your mind, Michael?" Her face was purple.

"What?"

"What are you thinking, she's a child. You could have been killed."

My dad didn't say anything, but you could tell he didn't

think it was that big a deal, which just made my mother even angrier. But we never flattened coins again.

The train came roaring past without slowing. Dust and dirt swirled and then everything was very still after the violence of the train. I looked around to see if anyone was looking and then I jumped back down onto the tracks. My penny and dime were still there, but now they were flattened, spread into oblong shapes. I picked them up and they had almost no weight. I tossed one in the air and caught it. It was so light, it was actually harder to catch than before, as if there was less gravity or something.

Down the track a ways were some kids. Boys. Four of them. And one of them with long hair and skinny arms was looking my way. I wasn't one hundred percent sure, but then when he kind of waved, very low and casual, I knew it was Simon.

I began to wander down the track in his direction, not as if I was headed there, but just moseying. The boys started down the embankment. They disappeared into the scrub between some buildings. I had never really considered Simon hanging out with other kids before. He seemed like such a loner that it was a weird idea.

I kept going in the same direction I had been traveling and about a minute later Simon popped back up onto the tracks. He looked once over his shoulder toward where the other kids had disappeared, and then he began to drift toward me.

I had never seen him outside of his house, and it was awkward for a minute or two as we stood around. He put one foot up on the railroad track.

"Watch out you don't get run over," I said.

"Yeah." He nodded, and sort of looked over his shoulder.

"Look at this," I said, and held out my flattened coins.

"What are they?" he asked.

"Haven't you ever flattened pennies?" I asked him.

"Not really," he said.

I explained all about how it was done, which, let's face it, wasn't very complicated. Simon nodded his head.

"Feel them," I said. "They're really light, which is weird, isn't it?" And I dropped them into the palm of his hand.

He kind of raised and lowered his hand a few times, as if he were really taking in the lack of weight.

"Cool," he said.

We heard a train coming from the other direction and scrambled over to the side and down the embankment. As we were settling into position with our chins just above the stones on the track level, Simon jumped up and slipped a little as he rushed up to the track. He plunged his hand into his pocket and stuck a coin on the rail. The train was closing in a lot faster than he probably thought it would. The whistle screamed.

"Hurry!" I called out to him.

Simon leaped out of the way, back toward me. He landed on the edge of the embankment, his elbows scraped on the stones. I saw him grimace, and he scrunched up close to me as the train roared past. My heart was pounding, the ground shook, and I could feel his breath on the side of my face.

Once the train was gone, we both started to laugh. The air was filled with dirt and flying dust, and we got up, rubbing our eyes. Simon walked back over to the track and retrieved his coin.

"Very cool," he said.

"That was a pretty close call," I said to him.

He shrugged. It was as if the shrug had been invented for his rubbery body.

"Let me see it," I said.

He held the coin out toward me and I took it. It was a penny, stretched out the way mine was, except for a tiny little extra tail on the end, kind of like a teardrop.

"You can have it," he said.

"No, it's yours." I handed it back.

I couldn't tell if he was disappointed I didn't take it.

"Actually," I said, "I'll take it. I mean, if you still want to give it to me."

Simon shrugged. "Sure," he said. He handed it to me—our fingers touched.

I put it in with my others.

"Thanks," I told him.

"You're welcome," he said.

We walked down the embankment, back in the direction of our houses.

Before long, it started to rain. I hadn't noticed it getting cloudy. Simon did not have an umbrella, and needless
to say, neither did I. I don't think I have ever carried an
umbrella in my life. I've always just gotten wet and soggy.
But in this particular case, it not only didn't matter, it just
made things better. We were completely soaked within a
few minutes. When I looked over at Simon, his hair was
all stringy and hanging down over his beautiful face. His
brow was scrunched up. He must have felt me looking at
him, because he turned to me—then he smiled. It was his
big goofy smile. It was in that instant that I knew I was in
love with Simon. I smiled back and we kept walking.

At the next corner we had to stop to let a car pass, and
when we stepped out into the street our hands just came
together—our fingers wrapped around each other's. After
a while, we started to swing our hands back and forth, just
a little bit with our walking; then we swung them really far
forward and back, up and down; then all the way around in
a giant circle. Then we started laughing. The rain kept coming down. We could not have gotten any more wet. It was
without question the happiest moment of my life. When we
finally got to the corner where I would turn off toward my
house, we stopped. I looked up into his eyes.

"See you tomorrow," he said.

"See ya tomorrow."

He leaned down to kiss me, right there on the street
corner, in public.

11

MOST MORNINGS I WOKE UP pretty happy, then after a few seconds it would hit me. Thomas. A weight would press down hard on my chest and it would be difficult to breathe for a few seconds until I got used to its being there for another day. Maybe I wouldn't have noticed it so much if I hadn't had the happiness with Simon in my life.

I'd never had a true boyfriend before, and having a really tall guy for the first one was spoiling me for life. I realized that right away. There was just something about the fact that he was so far up from the ground. It made me feel safe.

I had read something in one of Maxine's beauty magazines that people decide their type by the time they're two
years old. So, if as an infant you had a babysitter you liked a
lot who had blond hair, you would grow up to be attracted
to blonds. If I had been speaking to my parents I might have
asked if I had known any tall skinny guys when I was little.

The way Simon looked out over everything made him
seem very wise, and the fact that he didn't talk all that
much made him seem even more sage. When Simon did
say something, it was usually quite astute, except when it
was just totally ridiculous. He had a goofy side that I really
responded to. He made me laugh. It is a good thing to have
a fella who can make you laugh. Words of wisdom.

Simon had begun working as a junior counselor at this
weird study camp that his parents made him do. It was
like summer school, but supposedly more fun, with a lot
of time during the day for goofing off and playing sports.
From what I could tell, he didn't do a whole lot there, just
answer a question from some distracted kid every now and
then, and lie in the sun when they played dodgeball. He got
home around the same time as he normally would during
the school year, unless he missed the bus.

I didn't tell Simon about Thomas because I couldn't be
sure how he'd react. Granted, he was the most easygoing
person on the planet, but what if this was the straw that
broke the camel's back? Let's face it, everyone has one. What
if he suddenly thought I was a freak, or that my family was

a bunch of losers and he lumped me in with them? He and Maxine were basically the only good things in my life; the last thing I wanted to do was mess with that. There was just too much risk in revealing the truth.

And then one day while we were sitting on his futon, after a little kissing session, Simon pulled back from me.

"I want to see your room sometime."

"What? Where'd that come from?"

Simon started laughing. "You don't have to panic," he said.

"Well, you haven't seen my room," I said back. I was trying to be funny. Sort of. There was nothing all that wrong with my room, but between my parents and my sister, on top of the fact that my room was really not that interesting, there were just too many things that could go wrong.

But what could I do?

At dinner that night, I asked my dad how the real estate business was. He looked at me oddly. Granted, it was a question that was more than slightly out of the ordinary, especially lately.

"It's going fine, Lucy. Thank you for asking."

"You have a lot of showings?"

"I do," he said. He was still looking at me funny, but in a pleasant way. I'm sure he thought I was reaching out an olive branch or something of that nature.

I didn't know how to ask any more without making it totally obvious. Luckily, as my sister and I were cleaning the table after dinner, my dad told my mother that he had

a closing the next afternoon and would be a little late. My
mom told him that she had a meeting at four but would
be home by five thirty, after picking up my sister from her
rehearsal. So I had a few hours clear. I was set.

"I'll just head over to Maxine's," I threw in. There was
no reason for me to say it since that's what I did every day,
but I was so relieved that they would all be gone from the
house, it just came out.

I don't particularly care for being misleading, but let's
face it, with all the secrets I was keeping about this whole
thing, I was getting pretty good at not being all that direct.
Besides, desperate circumstances required desperate mea-
sures. Or maybe I'd just inherited a deceitful nature from
my father—who seemed suddenly in a very good mood.
Perhaps it was my showing interest in his affairs—no pun
intended. When I left the kitchen he was laughing, telling
my mom a story about a guy who bought a house as a surprise for his wife. That struck me as a very risky proposi-
tion; it wasn't like buying a scarf or even a car. You're stuck
with a house. I didn't hear the rest of the story because I
went up to my room to text Simon that we were on for the
next afternoon.

We met at his house and walked over to mine. I wanted
to make sure the coast was clear and not have him simply
show up in case something had changed. As we walked
over, I grew more and more nervous.

"Don't worry," Simon said. "I'm sure I'll love your room."

Then he smiled his goofy smile and took my hand and my stomach relaxed a bit. That's the kind of wisdom I'm talking about. He read my mind about the situation and made me feel at ease.

"Wow, I really like it," he said as he stood in the doorway to my room, taking in the scene. I noticed for the first time exactly how much junk I had gotten rid of. There was still no picture above the bed. I had been hoping to replace it with the cool painting of a golden eagle's head that was in our living room, but that would have required asking my mother.

"It's very Spartan," Simon said, reading my mind again.

Unlike his room, with the futon on the ground, there was no obvious place to sit in my bedroom except for the bed. I plopped on the edge while Simon walked around a bit. He spun my globe, then picked up the hand-woven hat from Peru on my shelf. The hat usually sat on top of the globe, but the night before Simon came over it struck me as cheesy that I had a hat on top of the world, so I plucked it off. As he fingered the cap, I was glad I had moved it. Then he did the craziest thing. When he went to set it down, he put it back on top of the globe.

He came and sat next to me on the bed. We started to kiss. It felt really weird to do that on my bed in my room in my house. But it also felt really nice after a minute. Then he put his hand over the zipper of my jeans. Neither one of us paid it any attention. It was as if it had fallen there by accident. He just left it where it was, and I certainly didn't move. We stopped kissing, and he pulled back but didn't move his hand from my pants.

"Thanks for bringing me over," he said.

I didn't know what to say, so I just said, "You're welcome."

He unsnapped the button to my jeans. I leaned back a little so he could unzip me. The whole process was kind of awkward, but he eventually got the zipper down most of the way. He put his hand in my underwear and just kind of rested it there. Then he started to move his fingers around a bit, but since the jeans were tight, there was only so far he could go. I would have to slide the pants down.

So I did.

I think this surprised me more than it did Simon, but not by much. I lifted my hips and pushed my pants down. They bunched up just above my knees. Then his finger reached inside me. I knew that my life would be changed from thereafter.

When Simon took his hand away, my brain wasn't working all that well, but I managed to stand and pull my pants up. I was glad to be in my room, glad it was with Simon, glad no one else was home. I was glad we had passed that milestone.

We hung out a little while longer, but I started to feel the pressure of time. Who really knew when anyone in my family might just walk in? Let's face it, they were all very unreliable.

"Shall we mosey on out of here?" I said.

Simon laughed. I didn't think it was that funny, but I was glad he liked it. I hopped up and clapped my hands. Simon just looked at me, then he jumped up and clapped his hands too.

"Alrighty," he said. When we got to my door, he turned back. "See ya, room."

Who says goodbye to an empty room? I mean, how charming was this guy?

"This is my sister's room," I said when we passed her door in the hall. I was just chattering, not really paying attention to what I was saying—I was so excited and distracted by what we had just done, and also relieved to be getting out of my house. "And that one is my parents.'" I was suddenly a tour guide.

"Your brother's room is downstairs?" Simon said at the end of the landing.

I froze.

Simon was three steps down the stairs before he noticed I wasn't beside him anymore.

"What is it?" He turned to me.

I couldn't speak.

"Are you okay?"

"Not really," I said.

"What's the matter?" He took a few steps back toward me. He was standing on the step below me so we were the same height, looking eye to eye.

"I have to show you something," I said at last. "Follow me."

Most other people would have nagged me about where we were going, but only once during the fifteen-minute walk did Simon ask what was happening.

"Just be patient, please," I said.

"Cool," he replied—God, I loved this man. But let's see if he would still love me after what I had to show him.

I led Simon to the bench directly across the street from Thomas's apartment where I had sat before. Simon looked around, trying to figure out what it was that I was being so secretive about. There was no one around. The cute little SUV wasn't in the parking lot.

"You see that apartment building across the street?" I asked him finally.

"Yup," Simon answered.

"That's where my brother's room is."

"What?"

"That's where he lives. With his mother, who isn't my mother." I explained about *the fling*.

Simon listened to every word I had to say, and then he was quiet for a while longer.

"What's his name?" he asked finally.

"Thomas."

"Really? My parents were going to name me Thomas if they hadn't named me Simon," he said.

"That's weird," I told him.

"But they didn't." He shrugged the Simon shrug. Then he got up and walked to the edge of the sidewalk and looked across at the building. I watched his back, and then went to stand next to him. His toes were dangling off the end of the curb. I did the same with mine, like we were at the end of a high diving board.

Simon just looked out toward the apartment the whole time. I had no idea what he was thinking.

"I just found out about it, not too long ago," I told him.

"You just found out about what?"

"That he existed."

"Wow," Simon whispered, in what qualified as the understatement of the year.

"Yeah." Then I told him about searching this place out and encountering Thomas that one time he was on his skateboard. Simon started to nod again and kind of stuck his lower lip out. His brow furrowed.

I was suddenly so sorry I had brought him, sorry I told him everything. My eyes were starting to burn—I wasn't going to be able to hold the tears in much longer. I wanted to run.

"I want to meet him," he said.

"You can't," I squealed. Apparently it was really loud, because he started to laugh. Then I started to laugh. And I couldn't stop. My laugh was hysterical, like a crazy person's. I just couldn't stop. Simon was still laughing a little, but not as much as I was, but he was smiling at me. Eventually he grabbed my shoulders and started shaking me.

"Stop laughing," he shouted into my face, but he was laughing now too. "Stop." Then he wrapped his long skinny arms around me and pulled me into a hug. I hadn't had any hugs in a long while. I had stopped letting my parents hug me after I found out about Thomas. And I don't think Simon had ever just hugged me before. We stood there, in the gutter, with his arms around me.

At some point I could feel that he was starting to pick his nails with his arms around me. "Stop picking your nails," I said as my laughter settled down.

"No," he said.

I laughed a little more at that and he did, too. We calmed down enough to sit on the curb. He looked over at me, and then reached out his arm to wipe my nose with his sleeve.

"Oh, that's gross," I said, and pulled my face away.

"No, it's not. It's what sleeves are for." He was looking at me with that goofy grin on his face.

That's when the SUV turned onto the street and pulled into the parking lot directly across from us.

Thomas hopped right out of the car, before the driver's-side door even opened. He was carrying a toy bow and arrow. His mother got out of the car with a food shopping bag in one hand and her purse in the other. She was prettier than I remembered that first time. Her light brown hair was pulled back in a ponytail; she wasn't skinny or fat, not too tall or very short. In fact, if she hadn't had sex with my father and then had a baby, I don't think I would have really noticed her at all.

Thomas had the arrow in position and the string of the bow was pulled back taut—he was ready to shoot. He spun around and pointed the weapon at his mother.

"Do not point that thing at me, Thomas," she scolded him. "I've told you that a thousand times. I will take it away if you do that again."

Why is it that all parents sound the same?

Thomas spun around and ducked behind the car and then pointed at some invisible target in the other direction.

"Go shoot it in the park, sweetie," his mother told him. She didn't even see us sitting right across the street. When she got to the door she called over her shoulder, "Dinner in half an hour," and went inside.

Thomas high-kicked like he was some kind of Ninja warrior, then grunted and spun and swung his other leg at some invisible foe.

I looked at Simon. He had that grin on his face again. "Watch out behind you!" he called out.

Thomas whipped around and saw us. He smiled.

"Behind you," Simon shouted again, and pointed at an invisible assassin.

Thomas whirled and pointed his arrow and let it fly. It

hit the outside of the apartment building and dropped into the bushes. He looked over his shoulder at Simon and then ran to retrieve it.

When he had the arrow again he put it back on the string and pulled it taut and started to march toward us. He had the largest, most diabolical grin on his face. When he got to the sidewalk across the street, he stopped. His toes were hanging over the curb, just like ours had been a few minutes earlier. The big black rubber tip of the arrow was pointed directly at Simon, who stood up beside me. "I dare you," he said.

Thomas giggled for just an instant and then fired. The arrow went zipping past Simon's head. Simon ducked, but if it had been on target it would have nailed him. No way he could have dodged it fast enough.

"Whoa," Simon said.

"Aw." Thomas groaned and went tearing down the street toward the dead end, then around onto our side of the street. He veered off the sidewalk onto the grass about twenty feet from us. As he was bending to get the arrow, Simon started to walk toward him.

"Can I see that thing?" Simon asked.

"Sure." Thomas held out the bow with one hand and the arrow with the other.

"This is totally cool," Simon told him. I don't know if he was a lonely kid or what, but Thomas was really pleased that this older guy thought something of his was so nice.

The two of them started to take turns shooting at a tree about twenty feet away. Simon was a very good shot, which is something I would not have expected. Not that I didn't think my boyfriend was athletic; it's simply that archery seems like a very specific thing, not something one just picked up and did very well at.

"Give it a shot," Simon said to me after he hit the tree for a third time in a row.

"Yeah," Thomas said. "Do you want to try it?"

I wasn't sure if he remembered me from the other time we met, but he didn't mention it. I did notice that he had blue eyes, which is something I hadn't registered the time I saw him. He had won the genetic battle that I had lost, the battle that saw me saddled with my mother's muddy brown eyes, while this kid got my dad's shiny blue peepers— illuminating once again how cruel and unfair life is.

I took the bow and arrow. Simon had to help me get the notch on the end of the arrow to sit on the string, but then I pulled it back. I missed the tree by about five feet.

"That's not too bad for a first try," Thomas said as he ran to get it. We took turns shooting for a few more minutes, until a second-story window in the apartment building across the street opened, and Thomas's mother called out.

"Dinner, Thomas."

"All right," he called back. Then turned to us. "I gotta go."

Simon held out his hand. "My name is Simon," he said.

"I'm Thomas," Thomas said, shaking Simon's hand. He

was acting very grown up. It's funny to see little kids shake hands; their grip is always so limp.

"And this is Lucy." Simon pointed at me.

"I know," Thomas said. "I met her before."

Thomas waved at us from two feet away, said, "See ya," then turned and ran down the street, around the dead end, then back up the other side of the street to his apartment. He pushed a button and turned to wave at us again. The buzzer buzzed, he spun back to the door, opened it, darted inside, and was gone.

The air was still.

We stood there for a bit and then began to walk up the street without speaking toward Prospect Avenue. I couldn't really focus on anything.

"He's a nice kid," Simon finally said.

I didn't say anything to that.

Simon took my hand as we crossed the avenue. I guess he could tell I wasn't in the mood, because once we got to the other side he released it and shoved his hands in his pockets. Even though I didn't want him to hold my hand, I almost started bawling my eyes out when he let go. I folded my arms across my chest and kept walking.

He was talking about some stupid research paper he had to do over the summer. Of all the times to talk about such an idiotic thing. I didn't even hear what the topic was. I was suddenly cold, even though it was hot out.

"Would you please just shut up," I said.

"Whoa." Simon's shoulders went up a bit and his hands went deeper into his pockets.

"Excuse me," I said, "but do you not think that it is just a tiny bit insane that I have a little brother, who I just found out about after EIGHT YEARS, who has no idea that the person he was just playing with is his sister?"

Simon shrugged.

"Don't just hunch your shoulders," I yelled at him. "What is the matter with you?"

Simon didn't say anything.

"What is the matter with everyone? This is not normal, this is not okay."

"It's just the way that it is," Simon said softly.

"It's not just the way that it is. Don't be such a fucking idiot," I yelled. I couldn't believe I was being this horrible to him, but I couldn't stop. "Do you have nothing more intelligent to say than that!"

Simon was speechless.

"What am I supposed to do here?" I demanded.

"I don't know, I guess," he mumbled to the ground.

"Figures," I scoffed. "I have to go home."

Simon didn't look at me. "Okay," he said.

I wished like crazy that he'd grab me and kiss me, or at least beg me to go back to his house, even though the last thing in the world I wanted was to sit on that stupid futon.

We stood on the corner for another second—then I turned and started walking toward home. When I was about ten feet away Simon called after me.

"It's not his fault, you know," he said. "It's not my fault, either."

This remark made me furious—even though somewhere I knew he was right. I couldn't even look over my shoulder. I knew if I did then I would say something I would regret, so I just kept walking.

12

____

SIMON TEXTED ME THAT NIGHT, asking if I was all right. Can you believe that? How amazing a person is Simon? I had treated him horribly and he reached out to me. But I couldn't answer. I just couldn't. I was so ashamed to have treated him like that, on top of which, I was still so angry. I didn't even know at who; everyone, I suppose. But now I wasn't talking to the only person in the world who understood me at all.

I didn't know what to do. It's not like we were in school and could run into each other in the hall or the cafeteria the next day—we would have said, "Hi," or something equally clever, and then it all would have been fine. And even if school was in session it wouldn't have mattered since we didn't even go to the same school.

I got a couple more texts from Simon—*R U there? Hello?*—but the worse I felt, the more difficult it was to respond to him. I was in a spiral. What a difference a day makes. Twenty-four hours earlier I had been sitting on the edge of my bed on the brink of losing my virginity with the man I loved (well, we had gone a lot further than I ever had before), and now here I was, sitting on the edge of that very same bed, totally alone on the planet.

I mentioned some time back that my mom had accused me of being a pessimist, but really, deep down, underneath it all, I have always had hope for a good life. I used to, anyway. This whole Thomas situation was unraveling everything. I needed to do something. I needed help. Bad.

I grabbed the phone. I hit Favorites and tapped Simon's name—right beside the ridiculous picture of him sticking his tongue out at the camera, a shot taken during happier times. Then I panicked. I hit the red button on the screen and ended the call before it connected. But the thing is, you can never be sure how quickly a call is disconnected on the other end. I've called people and then changed my mind before the phone has even rung, only to have them call me back in a few seconds and ask why I'd hung up.

My phone started buzzing. For a second, I let myself imagine that Simon must have been sitting on that futon waiting for my call and hit the call-back command right away. But when I looked down at my phone, it wasn't Simon calling. It was my dad.

I had to get out of my room. I dropped the phone on top of the dresser like it was molten lava. I pulled open the middle drawer of the dresser, reached in the back where I kept my secret money stash, grabbed a bunch, and was out the door in seconds flat.

I headed into town. I was going to buy a T-shirt I had seen in a window on Elm Street. I counted how much money I'd taken from my dresser— five twenties. More than I thought. I also had a five-dollar bill that was already in my pocket. Plus my flattened coins, which I guess weren't worth a damn. As I walked, I fingered the three flattened coins in my pocket. I had begun to carry them with me all the time—my two and the one Simon had given me. A mere remembrance of our once-flourishing relationship?

I was walking under the overpass that carried the train tracks, and then on a whim I veered off toward the railroad station. I told myself that it was a shortcut to the store—but I was heading back to the spot where Simon and I first became a couple, by the tracks where we flattened the pennies. Maybe it's stupid, but if I couldn't be with him, I wanted to at least feel close to him. Besides, there was never anyone around there.

When I arrived at the tracks I reached again for the flattened pennies in my pocket—they felt so frail, like they might break if I rubbed them too hard. So I stopped. I stood on the embankment, looking for the exact spot where Simon and I had lain together on the rocks while I felt his breath on me as that train roared past us. I couldn't find it. What was one of the most important shrines in my life was a dirty, unremarkable stretch of anonymous railroad track.

Far off, I could see a train coming. I stepped up to the tracks. Even in the daylight, the train's headlamp was bright. I looked down at the rails over which the steel wheels would roll in a few seconds. The train blew its whistle, as if it were yelling at me. I turned and watched it close in. I was only two steps from the track. The whistle screamed at me again. I looked straight up into the heavens. The sky was a dirty gray. The earth below my feet began to tremble. The train whistle screamed a third time. It was close now. What was I doing? I leapt back.

The train roared by as if it were furious with me. The wind it created shoved me back some more. Dust and dirt flew up around my face and into my eyes and throat. I began to choke. I coughed until tears rolled down my cheeks. I started spinning around and around in circles, I didn't know why. The rear of the train whooshed past. I became dizzy and stumbled and half fell, half sat on the small jagged rocks. Slowly, the turmoil around me began to subside and the air grew very still again. I could hear my breath.

I looked down the track and the train was nowhere in sight. It was long gone. I had been forgotten.

The station was not far in front of me. Inside, the air

was super stale. An old man sat on one of the long wooden benches reading a newspaper. Two people were buying tickets from the nearby machines.

Out on the platform five or six people were waiting. I looked up in the direction of where Simon and I had hung out and saw another train coming. The two people who had bought tickets from the machine came out. The train pulled slowly into the station and stopped. Maybe ten people got off. A conductor stepped out of the train and took off his hat. He brushed his hair back with his hand and stood beside the door while everyone on the platform got on board. Then the conductor looked up and down the track. He turned to look at me. I was only a few feet away, but I didn't think he had noticed me before.

"Going to New York, young lady?" he asked pleasantly.

"Oh," I said, "yes," and I got on the train.

I almost skipped on board. I turned left and went into the forward car. There were plenty of seats, but I walked to the very front of the car and then all the way to the back. The train started to gather speed and I was looking out the windows, left and right. Walking back up the aisle, swaying side to side with the motion, I felt giddy. I ended up on the left side, in a window seat, near the front, for no reason.

I had taken the train into the city only a few times in my entire life. Once when my dad's car was broken and we were going to the circus, and another time when my mom took my sister and me to see a matinee. And one other time when some friends and I went ice-skating at Rockefeller Center. Otherwise, my dad drove us—not that we went into the city all that much.

Trains are very pleasant, except for the fact that very few things actually face the railroad tracks, so, consequently, you are usually looking at the back of people's lives. And people throw a lot of junk out the back of the buildings. My view was scarred by their debris. The redeeming thing about all this, however, is that the scenery moves by so quickly on a train. The instant after you see some rusted car or empty, derelict swimming pool—things that were originally intended to bring joy—the view changes and you can forget all about the sorry sight and take in the next little disappointment that life out your window has to offer.

It was good to be in motion.

The same conductor who invited me onto the train came down the aisle, collecting tickets, which of course I didn't have.

"I can sell you one," the conductor said. "But it's five dollars more than if you'd bought it at the station."

"Oh," I said. "Well, okay," and gave him one of my five twenties.

"Round-trip is twenty-six dollars." He wasn't as nice as he had been when I was getting on.

"I know," I said quickly. I didn't want him to think I didn't know what I was doing. "I just need a one way."

He nodded. "Thirteen seventy-five." He ripped out the

ticket, punched it with his old-fashioned hole puncher, shoved a piece of paper into the slot on the top of the seat in front of me, and handed me my change and the receipt.

"I didn't charge you the surcharge," he said.

"Thanks," I said.

He winked at me and moved up the aisle. I generally don't like winks all that much. They tend to be pretty cheesy, but he was very good at it. It was almost as if I couldn't be sure he had actually winked, it was that subtle—perhaps the best wink I've ever gotten.

Things out the window began to look grittier, grungier. There were refineries and big oil storage tanks. It all looked rather dingy, even the different colored cargo containers that were piled up. I didn't care. Finally the train went underground into a tunnel. Then while we were still moving through the darkness, people started lining up in the aisle to get off. They just couldn't wait to hit the city.

I let most everyone leave the train before me. I nodded as they passed me, giving out what I hoped was a mysterious look of satisfaction—my Mona Lisa smile. I actually didn't know what the hell I was doing, or where I was going to go now that the train had reached its destination.

I followed the other passengers up the broken escalator. Why is it that broken escalators are harder to climb than regular stairs?

The station was huge; I didn't recognize it at all. There were fast-food restaurants selling pizza and donuts, pretzels, and Mexican food; newsstands with billions of magazines; and signs all over the place—for stores, train tracks, waiting areas. Arrows pointed toward the subway—I didn't know anything about the subway or what the different colors and numbers meant—some of the signs had arrows pointing two directions for the same subway. People swarmed in all directions. A big board was showing various train departures, clicking and changing all the time. A crowd of people stood under it craning their necks. I wandered down a long hall, to another part of the station where there was another board with different train information changing every few seconds.

I looked up at it for a while. I couldn't decipher it at all. I didn't want to ask anyone for help. For the first time since I'd left home, I really wished I had my phone. I could picture it in my mind, sitting on the corner of my dresser—a million miles away.

I saw a red sign for an exit and walked up another escalator that didn't work—and suddenly I was outside. If I thought it was bad in the station, it was complete chaos out here. It was beginning to get dark and cars had their lights on. The street right in front of me was bumper-to-bumper traffic; trucks were honking their horns. Someone jostled me into someone else going the other direction. My shoulder got slammed pretty hard, and I didn't even see into who I had been shoved. I stumbled out of the flow of people rushing in and out of the station and it was slightly less chaotic—not calm, but at least I wasn't getting run over. A long line of people was waiting to get into taxis pulling up by the curb.

Up at the corner, a mass of humanity raced across the street, while another herd of people waited for the light to change in the other direction. Brightly lit signs announced the stores all along the block. I saw the sign for Macy's. It was old-fashioned and it didn't light up—there was just an arrow underneath the name, pointing the way. I was in Macy's once as a kid, with my parents. We went to see Santa—which I hated—and my sister got lost. It was a real disaster trying to find her. The last thing I needed was to get trapped in the biggest store in the world.

Then something flashed in my brain—a sign I had seen back in the station. Why I suddenly remembered it, why it jumped into my mind at that instant when I had no memory of even noticing it in the first place, I can't explain.

I had been looking at so many things, but the sign and poster must have subconsciously registered in my overworked brain. On it was a painting of a train rushing past a lighthouse. Overlapping that was a picture of a happy family—mother and father, child and grandfather. And a list of destinations for the Downeaster, the train to Maine.

I slithered through the crowd and made it back to the station. I walked down another broken escalator and marched right up to the poster. It said what I had thought it had said. The train went to Maine. That's where I was going.

Suddenly and without question, I was going to Maine to see my grandfather.

The ticket counter was off to my left and the line wasn't too bad.

"I'd like a ticket for the Downeaster, please," I said to the woman behind the glass.

"The what?"

"The Downeaster, the train to Maine."

"Sweetie, there's no train to Maine from here—oh wait, you want that tourist train. Honey, you get that in Boston. You have to go to Boston first and self-transfer there from Back Bay to North Station. But I can sell you the whole thing if you like. Next train in twelve minutes."

I couldn't really follow what she was saying, but I said, "Sure, that sounds good. How much is it?"

She slapped a few keys on her computer. Her nails were very long and very red. I don't know how she hit the keys without breaking those nails.

"It's $136 one way, sweetie."

I had a little more than ninety dollars left. She must have seen my face drop because very quickly she said, "You know, you can go over to the Port Authority and get yourself on the bus. That'd be a lot cheaper."

"Okay, where's that?"

"Sweetie, you can take the C or the E train one level down, or you can go out to Eighth Avenue and just walk uptown—same direction as the traffic—to Forty-Second Street. You can't miss it."

"This way?" I pointed behind me, to where I had just come in.

"That's Seventh Avenue. Go down that hall to the other end and go up the escalator and you'll be on Eighth."

And that's what I did. I went down the hall, up an escalator that actually worked, and started walking in the same direction the cars were going. For the first time the thought of just going home occurred to me. But what would I do once I got there? I couldn't call Simon, not after the way I treated him, and then ghosting him like I had. And why had my father been calling me? He never calls me unless there's a problem; he always texts—my mother teases him that it's his way of staying young. I was pretty sure the call had something to do with my visit to Thomas. I kept walking. Ahead I saw a massive building with a giant overhang. Taxis were double-parked, horns honked. People were crossing the street between cars.

"This must be the place," I actually said out loud, like I was in a movie or something.

Under the huge, ugly portico, people were swarming. My toes got run over by a large wheelie bag. The person pulling it didn't even notice. I walked through the glass doors and right in front of me there was an information booth, but no one was working at it. Another huge crowd of people milled about, and the same junky restaurants that I had seen at the train station lined the halls. There were also a lot of people just hanging around, not going anywhere. This place was similar to the train station, but a little seedier—to use one of my dad's words.

I walked over to a newsstand. The man behind the counter looked like he might have been from India. "Do you know where I get tickets for Greyhound buses?" I asked him. I had no idea if Greyhound was what I wanted, but they were the only bus company I knew.

"Downstairs," he said in a beautiful singsong accent, pointing toward an escalator that I hadn't noticed. "There."

I started to walk away from the counter—then I turned back. "Where are you from?" I asked him.

"I am from Bangladesh," the man said in his singsong.

If that's what everyone in Bangladesh sounded like, then it was a place I wanted to visit soon, even if I had no idea where it was. I waved my thanks; the man smiled brightly.

"Have a safe trip," he called after me.

The Greyhound office was on the right at the bottom of the escalator. There was that great sign with the skinny dog all stretched out, looking as if he was running really fast. I was so happy to see that sign that I ran off the escalator. I smacked right into an old lady.

"Watch it!" she shouted at me, stumbling back.

"Oh, I'm so sorry," I said to her, and reached out my arms toward her. She pulled away from me like I had Ebola, and muttered something. I wasn't sure exactly what she said, but it definitely contained the word "fucker."

I burst into tears. I had no idea that was coming. I tried to stop it right away—the last thing I needed was to be crying in the middle of the bus station in New York, with all sorts of child poachers and derelicts hiding close by. It took me a minute to settle back down. I kept my face low and wiped my tears. I glanced around, but no one seemed to have noticed me. There were two agents behind the counter and I slowly approached the one that didn't have anyone buying a ticket. The counter was high, and since I'm height deprived, my chin was basically touching the top of it. I rubbed my eyes and made a show of being tired so that he wouldn't think my eyes were red from crying.

"How much is a ticket to Maine?" I asked the man behind the counter.

He had black hair plastered down to his head. His part was crooked. He wore large black glasses that made his eyes seem very large. "To where, to Portland?"

"In Maine, yeah," I said.

"Round-trip or one way?"

"Um, how much is a round-trip?"

He looked at the screen on his computer. "A hundred and eleven dollars and fifty cents," he said.

"Oh." I heard my voice and it sounded very small.

I needn't have worried about him noticing if I'd been crying; the guy was a zombie.

Maybe my grandfather would pay for my return—or maybe I would never return.

"And for a one-way ticket?"

"Fifty-eight dollars and fifty cents. It's only forty-five if you buy it online." His voice went up at the end of his sentence, like I ought to have done that. It was the one sign of life he showed.

"What time does it leave?"

He looked at the screen again. Everything was a great effort for him. "Next bus leaves at four a.m. There's one after that at eleven fifteen tomorrow. You have to change in Boston on either one." He looked at me.

I could tell my mouth was kind of hanging open.

I bought a ticket for the 4 a.m. bus. That left me with $32.75. I could have gone back to Penn Station and gotten a train back home, but I was on my way now. The hard part was done. I had my ticket. I had a destination. The open road was before me. Besides, there was nothing for me back home but trouble and loneliness. I was going to my grandfather's house. I was going—I had always been going. I had nearly nine hours to kill before the bus.

It would be dinnertime at my house, but there would be no dinner. My parents would be extremely worried about me at this point. I had never disappeared like this before. I considered calling them from a pay phone. I wanted to send word that I was okay so they wouldn't worry or call the police to come track me down or anything, but I didn't

want to talk to them. I needed to send an email. The Port
Authority was at Forty-Second Street. That big library with
the lions out front was on Forty-Second Street. How did I
know that? I just did.

Instead of going out the way I came in, I ended up taking the escalator back up and walking through the whole
building and heading out onto Ninth Avenue. It was fully
dark now. The street was backed up; cars were lined up
under signs for the Lincoln Tunnel back to New Jersey.
Three cranes dotted the sky and dirty fences lined the street
at two side-by-side construction sites. The sidewalk was
closed, so pedestrians were pushed out into the street in
makeshift walkways behind orange cones. I turned right,
toward the corner of Forty-Second Street. Before I even got
there, I passed this place with two old-fashioned computers sitting on the counter by the window. A sign next to the
computers said, "Internet cafe." Inside, a not-so-friendly
guy behind the counter sold me a slip of paper with the
login information on it. And I bought a Coke. In all, it cost
me $6.50 for the soda and a half hour on the computer. I
had $26.25.

Dear Mom, I wrote. *Don't worry, I'm fine. I've just
decided to take a small road trip. I will let you know
when I get to where I'm going, it's a surprise. It will
especially be a surprise for Dad. I'm sorry I didn't tell
you in advance, but I'm doing well and hope you are*

too. Please don't worry or be mad. I'll contact you soon. Love, Lucy. And I pressed send.

Then I sat and finished my Coke and watched people walk past the window. I was in no rush, that was for sure.

My stomach started grumbling. I was starving—actually, I shouldn't say starving. I hate when people say that. I was in no way starving like people in Central America or Africa might be, but I was quite hungry. I had been so busy up to now that I hadn't noticed—I hadn't really eaten since breakfast. A little bit up the block and across the street was a pizza place that sold slices for a dollar—ninety-nine cents to be exact. I could see that I was not in a great neighborhood and the pizza place had nowhere to go in and sit down, just a window on the street where you got the slices. There were a lot of not-so-friendly-looking guys hanging out in front. But I had to eat.

I stepped up to the window and ordered a slice, and by the time I got back to the corner, I had eaten it all. The place may have been funky, but the pizza was super hot and tasty. I turned around and went back for another slice. There was a small line now. While I was waiting, a guy in a hoodie noticed me.

"Hey, girly girl. You like pizza?"

"Um, yeah," I mumbled.

He must not have heard me because he said, "Yo, I'm talking to you, young lady. Are you deaf, princess?"

I don't know if he was being mean or funny or what, but it got the attention of a few other people who I could feel turn toward me. My turn came at the window.

"One," I said, holding up a finger. And I gave the pizza man a dollar.

One of the guys who had just noticed me came over. "Can you spare a dollar?"

I looked at him. Where his eyes should have been white, they were yellow. There was pus-like stuff in the corners.

Another guy shoved the guy with yellow eyes and said, "Leave her alone, man. Get outta here." Then he grabbed for him. The first guy jerked his shoulder away. His arm went flying. He missed my face by an inch but his hand caught my shoulder pretty hard. I stumbled back and crashed into another guy. He spilled his Coke on the ground.

"What the fuck, man!" The guy with the Coke threw his free hand up in the air. Yellow Eyes slammed him into the wall. Out of the corner of my eye I could see the pizza guy ignoring it all, still holding my slice. The guy who had been shoved into the wall started screaming at the guy with the yellow eyes and got up in his face, real close. Everyone started closing in, cursing, screaming. I turned and saw a taxi, stuck in traffic. I lunged between Yellow Eyes and the other guy and dove to get in that car. I slammed the door behind me and pushed down the lock in one move. It was quiet. But not for long.

"Where you going?" the driver shouted over his shoulder.

"Um, nowhere really," I kind of mumbled. "I just had to—"

"What?" he barked.

"I don't need to go anywhere," I yelled to the driver through the Plexiglas partition that separated the passenger seat from the driver. "I'll just get out." I reached for the door handle on the side away from the trouble.

"I already started the meter," the driver shouted.

"Sorry," I said.

"You owe me four dollars."

"What?" I said.

"You get in, I start the meter, that's how it works."

"But I just got in to get away from those guys. I didn't—"

"You get in, you pay." He had turned around to face me. There was a throbbing vein on the side of his forehead. I couldn't tell if he was really angry or if he just had to shout through the Plexiglas. "Four dollars."

I reached into my pocket and grabbed the first bill I touched. I shoved it into the tray cut into the Plexiglas and reached for the door. It was locked.

"Hey!" I shouted at the driver. "Open the door!" I was trapped.

The driver pushed a dollar back into the tray.

In my rush to get out I had forgotten my change. I grabbed for it. He popped the lock and I flung the door open. I now had $20.25 left, and I hadn't even gotten out of New York.

JUST FLY AWAY 125

I got out of the cab on the street side, away from the pizza place. The driver yelled at me not to get out that way, but I slammed the door on him. My heart was pounding almost out of my chest. The taxi hadn't even moved more than ten feet from where I got in. I cut across the street. When I was almost to the other side I looked over my shoulder. The altercation at the pizza place had settled down, and things looked pretty much as they had before I went over. Nobody was thinking about me. I hadn't even gotten my second slice of pizza that I paid for.

I started screaming, really loud. I just stood there on the sidewalk and let it rip. What was funny was that since it was already so loud on the street, with all the cars honking and the trucks and buses and everything else, my scream really didn't seem that loud. I did it again. A few people walking by looked at me as if I was strange, but by the third scream I started laughing. A lady walked by with a little boy, maybe three or four years old, and when the kid saw me screaming, he screamed, too. Then we were both screaming and laughing.

The mother pulled the boy away by his wrist. "Felix!" she scolded him.

Some people are so uptight.

13

THE BUS STATION WAS MUCH LARGER than it first seemed—
and it had felt huge from the start. An overpass above the
street connected an entire other building, much bigger
than the first one. Both buildings were dingy.

There was even a bowling alley in the upstairs corner
of the bigger building. I thought it would have been nice to
watch a little bowling while I waited for my bus, but it was
not to be. The bowling alley had a bar, and since it was after
8 p.m., they wouldn't let me in.

I went down to the Bangladesh man's newsstand again,
but it was closed. Nearby there was another newsstand, not
as neatly organized, and I flipped through magazines for

a long time, until it looked like the guy behind the counter was going to say something to me. My friend with the
beautiful singsong accent would have let me read all night
long, I'm sure.

I was still hungry. Across the way was a little stand
selling snacks. The donuts in the glass case looked to me
like scared mouths crying "oovoo!" Their glazed frosting
was a bit crusty, as if they had been there quite a while. I
wanted one anyway, but my cash was draining fast, so decided against the donut. I was furious with that guy who
had shoved me and started the whole fight so that I couldn't
get my second slice of pizza.

The station began to thin out. There were more weirdos
and homeless people as time went on. Perhaps they had
always been there, and it was just that when things got less
crowded I simply noticed them more. One guy in particular was engaged in a pretty heated discussion with someone
who had done him a serious wrong; the only problem was
that the other guy wasn't there.

There was a small waiting area right beside Gate 83, my
gate, but a homeless guy was sleeping stretched out across
a row of chairs, all his stuff piled up next to him in garbage
bags. He smelled pretty bad. I sat on the ground by the
door. I figured just in case I fell asleep, the bus driver would
nudge me.

I was tired, but I didn't doze. My mind wandered.
Thoughts kept returning to my sister. I'm not someone who

misses people as a general rule. Even as a kid, when I was away at camp, as other people were quietly, or not so quietly, weeping into their pillows, I was totally fine. I never wasted a second being homesick, but I was sitting there missing Julie for some reason. I was thinking about how, when we were a lot younger, we used to play these crazy imagination games, for hours, about living on another planet. I hadn't thought of that in a long time.

Then I must have fallen asleep for I don't know how long, but when I woke up, the bus still hadn't arrived. The room around me was quiet; almost everyone I could see was asleep. Those who weren't were just staring off, waiting for a bus or for morning. I had no idea what time it was. For the first time all night, I was scared. This whole trip suddenly seemed like a really bad idea. I could feel myself starting to panic. There was a pay phone by the escalator. I dug into my pockets and found some change.

I almost couldn't remember Simon's number. When I did, the call went right to his voice mail. "Hey, it's Simon here," his silky voice said. My shoulders dropped and my eyes welled up. "Leave me a message if that's your thing, and I'll get back at you when I'm free." Then the phone beeped. I stood there holding the dirty receiver—who knows how many people had clutched this same phone, making that one last call to a loved one before they set off for God knows where. Eventually I hung up without leaving a message. What was there to say—except everything.

Back over at my gate there was activity. A sleepy-looking man in a gray uniform was moving the stanchion away from the door. He had a small moustache and a very large stomach. He told me they would be boarding in a few minutes. About fifteen people gathered around the gate. Everyone was moving pretty slow. A lot of the people had suitcases, and for the first time it occurred to me that I didn't even have a toothbrush.

Instead of having a Greyhound on the side, the bus was painted green and said *Peter Pan,* with a little flying guy in a lame hat hovering between the words *Peter* and *Pan.* I asked the driver if I was at the wrong bus—that's all I needed after all this waiting.

"The companies merged. You'll get a Greyhound in Boston," he explained. He was fairly pleasant for the middle of the night. I took one more look at the little Peter Pan guy on the side of the bus. I hate that Peter Pan story. I could never understand how someone wanted to stay a child his whole life. I'm sorry, but I cannot relate. Ever since I was very little I've wanted to be older.

I took a seat about halfway back on the bus, by a window. It was a huge relief to be on board. I think I was asleep before we had pulled out of the station.

I felt the bus stop a few times, and at one point I could feel someone come and sit next to me, but nothing could have woken me up until the driver shook me by my shoulder.

"You have to change buses," he said. "We're in Boston."

"Already?" I was instantly wide-awake. "Okay, thanks." The bus was empty and I got off fast.

I had never been to Boston before, but after the bus station in New York, Boston was a breeze. This place was beautiful. There was a giant circular skylight in the center of the ceiling; it looked like a flying saucer was about to land on your head. You really felt like you were arriving somewhere special. And more important at the moment, it had a shop called Honey Dew Donuts, which I had never heard of before. I am generally not a donut person; they are not something I usually spend much time considering. But since New York, when I didn't buy one because I was trying to save money, I had been itching for a taste.

I had three.

At 99 cents apiece, they were worth every penny. I shall never forget those honey- dipped beauties. I was, in that instant, as content as I can remember being in a long while. I had the simple pleasure of superb junk food in my stomach, half my journey completed and an exciting half to go.

There was only an hour between buses, and I had to hustle if I was going to make it. I really enjoyed Boston. I would definitely come back and see more of it. I found my next bus and was back on the road.

I sat up front so I could see out the windshield. Once we cleared the city, and then the suburbs, it didn't take all that long till we passed a sign welcoming us to New Hampshire.

The vista was all tall evergreen trees on both sides for as far as the eye could see. I know next to nothing about trees, but these looked very much like the one that grows in the middle of our deck back home, under which I was sitting when I found out about Thomas.

There was a big deal made about that particular tree a number of years back when my parents were about to build the deck. At first they were going to chop down the tree but then my dad had a fit, saying that the whole atmosphere would be ruined if the tree was gone. So then he decided to just not build the deck, and my mom was really upset about it. She didn't say anything for three days. Did not speak. It was very bizarre.

Looking out the window now, I wondered if those trees were plagued with as much sap as that tree back home, and it occurred to me that maybe my mom being so upset back then was really not about the deck. From what they had told us, it would have been right around this time that she learned about Thomas. Perhaps that's what her silent treatment had really been about.

The deck situation was rescued by my sister—believe it or not—who was around eight herself at the time. "Why don't you cut a hole in the deck and let the tree stay there?" she said one day out of the blue.

From the mouth of babes, right?

So that's what they did. I have to say, it was a pretty brilliant idea. My parents decided to make the deck even bigger, and to this day there is this giant tree growing right up out of the middle of it.

After what seemed not too long a time, there were trees on both sides of the road as far as the eye could see. For some reason I started thinking about the fight outside the pizza place again. It was hard to get the image of that guy with the yellow eyes out of my head. I think it had freaked me out even more than I thought at the time. I hate to admit it, but I honestly wondered if I was more afraid of him because he was an African American than I would have been if he'd been a white guy. Does even asking the question make me a racist? I know you're not supposed to think stuff like that, let alone say it out loud—but how are we supposed to figure it out? I'm sorry, but this whole race thing is something I feel bad about; all these feelings everybody has about everybody else, although half the time we don't even know we have them, or want to have them, while we all try to do our best. I don't know how it will be resolved, at least in my generation.

While my mind was wandering around all this, a sign caught my eye out the window—we were in Maine, just like that. Wow. I started laughing.

That was easy, I thought. But then my stomach started to feel a little queasy. Maybe it was due to riding for so long, but I was also getting a little worried. I really started to wish I had my phone. As I said, I'm not that into looking at the phone every thirty seconds, but there are times when it's better company than whatever is on your mind. In this particular instance, what I began to think about, and couldn't stop thinking about, was the fact that I didn't really know my grandfather at all. I began to wonder if I'd even recognize him. Or would he be mad that I just showed up on his front lawn unannounced? And since I would be almost out of cash, with no means to get back, I started to become concerned.

Although, I have to say, Harold—that's my grandfather's name—did seem to like me when he met me. He kept calling me Lulu and would raise his voice on the second part, so it sounded like *LuLU*. No one had ever called me by a nickname before, and I was surprised by how much I liked it. My dad said that his father only had nicknames for people he really liked. Perhaps that's what had made me kind of partial to my grandfather –that and his love for ice cream.

At one point, I got up to go to the bathroom in the back of the bus. Somebody had missed and the toilet seat was a mess. I decided to hold it, and when I returned to my seat the lady across the aisle started talking to me. Up until now she had not made a peep. I didn't think she had even noticed me—and now she was talking as if we had been having a conversation the whole time.

She wanted to know my name and how old I was and where I was headed. I told her I was going to Bennelton.

"I make the trip fairly often," I said, "so it's no big deal."

"Well you certainly seem very mature for someone so young."

I liked her right away. She had the old-lady voice, kind of frail and trilly, and her face had ten thousand lines on it. She was so wrinkled that you could almost not even tell she had wrinkles. But the wrinkles made her kind of beautiful also, as if she was the oldest person on the planet.

"Your grandfather is very lucky to have such a devoted granddaughter. Such a long journey."

"Well, we're very close," I went on. I was making up stuff left and right. "We always have been."

She looked directly into my eyes every time I spoke. She nodded her head carefully, as if she were attempting to understand something complicated, instead of my crazy fabrications about how I was accustomed to travel and all the hardships it entailed.

"So when you get to Portland, you know you have to go over to the Transportation Center."

"Oh, yeah," I told her. "That's no problem; do it all the time." I was really getting up a good head of steam.

She told me that her son-in-law was picking her up in Portland and they would drop me off at the station. She didn't ask me if they could give me a lift; she just told me that that's what was going to happen. It felt nice.

"I just love Robert," she said. "That's his name, Robert, not Bob." Her own daughter was difficult, she said. And that was the word she used, *difficult*, but not Robert; he was a dreamboat. It felt a bit awkward to hear such an old lady call someone a dreamboat but it sounded like it was a word from her era, so it fit.

Sure enough her son-in-law was waiting right outside the bus when it pulled up to the curb at the Portland station. I would not have qualified him as a dreamboat. He was a bit chubby and moved kind of slow, but I imagine her qualifications for dreamboat were different than mine. He was a very polite man and in a few short minutes I was deposited outside the Transportation Center. I insisted that I knew exactly where I was going and marched inside with a wave over my shoulder.

Once I was through the door I raced for the bathroom. This may not sound very delicate, but sometimes taking a pee is one of the most satisfying things a person can do. But then once I walked back out into the station I felt lost. It's not that the place was so big; compared to the other two I had been in it should have been no sweat, and it wasn't busy at all; it's just that I hadn't really thought what would happen after I got this far. I had somehow figured that once I was in Maine that would be it.

By now I did have some experience on the road, so I walked up to the information counter in the corner and inquired how I might get to Bennelton and how far the trip was.

There was a Concord Coach leaving for Rockport, which was ten miles from Bennelton, at 12:15 p.m. I looked up at the clock over on the back wall of the information booth and saw that it was not even noon. I started laughing. For some reason the fact that I was here in Maine before noon amazed me. This time yesterday I was still in New Jersey. I hadn't yet brought Simon to my house, or to meet Thomas, or had a big fight. What a twenty-four hours.

I bought a ticket for $8.50 and headed toward the bus idling out front.

I considered telling the bus driver, who was standing beside the bus chatting with two other men, that he was causing a lot of pollution and wasting gas at the same time, but a sign across the road proclaiming *Only $7.50 for the Best Crab Cakes in Maine* caught my eye. Instead of yelling at the driver I asked him if that was true.

"I don't know if they're the best," he said in an accent that reminded me of the woman at the Boston donut counter, "but they're wicked good."

I'd had crab cakes before, down the shore, but even so, the image I always get in my mind when I hear *crab cakes* is a birthday cake with vanilla frosting and lots of crab claws sticking out the sides.

"Better hurry," the driver said. "We're leaving in ten minutes."

These crab cakes of course looked nothing like a birthday cake. Maybe it was the spicy mayo, but they were indeed wicked good. Wicked was officially my new favorite word.

14

BY NOW I WAS SICK AND TIRED of getting on buses. But I took my seat in the front row again, and then, without realizing it, I fell fast asleep.

I had the strangest dream. I was boarding a plane with Simon. We were walking down that portable hallway that connects the terminal to the plane. Just as I was stepping on board I softly kicked the outside of the plane three times for luck. I wasn't sure where we were going, but the flight attendant greeting everyone as we got on was very friendly and pointed us toward the back of the plane. As the plane started to take off I realized I was terrified of flying. I clutched Simon's hand really hard and he laughed. I could see out of the corner of my eye that he was looking at me with that goofy grin of his.

Then we were up in the cockpit and flying the plane. But it wasn't a giant passenger jet like the one we had boarded; instead, it was a tiny two-seater propeller plane. We were both holding those airplane steering wheels, not the full-circle ones in cars, but the kind that are half wheels with no top and bottom, only sides. I wasn't sure which one of us was actually flying and who was the copilot, but we pulled back on the wheels and we went up through the clouds.

Then we were outside the plane and bouncing on the clouds as if they were giant fluffy trampolines. What a feeling! If there is a definition of the word *joy*, bouncing on those clouds would be it. In the dream, I realized I had never truly experienced joy until that instant, and now that I had, nothing would ever be the same again. But it didn't last long.

Soon we were back in the cockpit, but it was a giant plane now and we were flying incredibly close to the ground, first through the country between lots of trees, then in a city. We had to keep tipping the plane way over on its side to avoid the wings hitting trees and the buildings lining the narrow streets we were flying through. We had to fly under low bridges. It was terrifying. It was all coming at us so fast. Then we landed the plane just outside of the town—on a small road. Everyone hurried off like the plane was going to catch fire; none of the passengers said thank you to us for saving them with such daredevil flying. As we were walking into the town, I realized we were in a foreign country where no one spoke my language.

Then I woke up. I'm not much of a dream interpreter, so I didn't try, but my forehead was kind of clammy, though it might have been from the sun.

The ocean was right out my window. The coast was rocky, not at all like the Jersey shore. I thought it would be fun to be floating in the water with all the seagulls diving into the ocean around me as they looked for lunch. After a few minutes I leaned forward and asked the driver how long till we got to Rockport.

He turned and stared at me for a second. "We passed Rockport about fifteen minutes ago. I called it out; how'd you miss it?"

"I guess I was sleeping," I mumbled.

"You can get off at Belfast in about twenty minutes and get a bus back." The driver didn't seem that concerned with my plight.

"When is there a bus going back?" I could hear that my voice was high and shrill.

"You'll have to ask there." He shrugged, and was basically done with me.

Maybe I was just getting sick and tired of traveling, or maybe it was because I was almost out of money and didn't know what I'd do once it was gone, or perhaps it was because the whole thing was starting to seem like a stupid idea, but the ocean out the window now looked like a cold and not very nice place to swim. The last thing I needed on top of everything else was to have seagulls pooping all over my head as I bobbed up and down trying not to drown in the undertow or get dashed against the rocks.

I reached into my pocket and pulled out the flattened coin Simon had given me, the one with the little teardrop at the end. I rubbed it, turning it over and over in my hand— but I had to put it away. I was going to start crying if I kept that up. There are times in life when it feels nice to be sad and lonely—this was not one of them.

Just as it was beginning to seem as if I was never going to get anywhere, we pulled into the bus station in Belfast, except it was not a bus station at all. It was a Shell gas station with a very appropriately named Dead River Convenience store attached to it. It was already 2:30 and the next bus back wasn't until 6 p.m. I had a grand total of $1.28 left. A ticket back to Rockport was $5.25. Out the window I could see a bench by the side of the road. I bought a Coke for a dollar and went to sit on it to review my situation.

I was basically broke. I had no means of getting any- where. I had no means of communication. No one in the world knew where I was—which, if it hadn't been for my current situation, would have been a feeling I liked. I was stuck. I finished my soda and concluded that my situation sucked.

JUST FLY AWAY 141

I was about to go back inside and explain this to the guy behind the counter and see if he would let me ride back for free since I had simply missed my stop and had no intention of ending up in Belfast, when a red pickup truck that had been filling up at the pump pulled over to me. The guy behind the wheel had a mesh baseball cap. He leaned across the seat and rolled down the passenger window and shouted out to me.

"Where you headed?" He had a shaggy beard and greasy hair.

Of course I had been taught all about not getting into cars with people I didn't know. If there's one thing my parents and schools drummed into me from a young age, it's stranger danger. For whatever reason, I didn't think of any of that at the moment. I was broke, I was tired, and I needed a lift.

"Bennelton," I said.

"I'm headed that way." The guy scratched his beard. "Hop in."

I got off the bench and started toward the pickup. As I was reaching for the door it vaguely passed through my mind that I was doing something not very smart. I popped the handle and climbed in. There were dirty old newspapers scattered on the floor under some rubber boots and a pair of yellow waterproof overalls. He must have been a fisherman or something. On the dashboard was a pack of

Marlboro Light cigarettes. Reflected in the windshield was the cigarettes' warning label. "SMOKING KILLS," it said in big black letters.

The driver pulled out onto the road. There was a funny smell inside, but I couldn't place what it was.

"You live in Bennelton?" he asked.

"Um, no. My grandfather does," I said. "But I visit here a lot."

I was looking straight ahead. Out of the corner of my eye I could see the guy glance over at me. The stoplight in front of us was changing from green to yellow. We probably could have made it through before it turned red, but he slowed down.

"Bennelton's a nice town," he said. "Quiet."

"Yup. That's the way we like it."

When we stopped at the light, he reached for the pack of cigarettes on the dash and shook it with a flick of his wrist. A single cigarette popped out an inch or so—it was a smooth move, I'll give him that. He lifted the pack to his mouth and plucked the cigarette with his teeth.

I looked over at the guy and he smiled, the cigarette dangling between his lips.

"You don't care if I smoke?"

"No business of mine," I said back at him.

He reached between us into the crack of the seat and dug out a blue plastic lighter.

"What's your name?" he asked me as the tip of his cigarette flamed.

"Monica," I lied.

"How old are you, Monica?"

"Seventeen," I lied again.

He nodded his head and made a clicking sound between his teeth. The traffic light in the other direction
turned yellow. I snapped that door handle open and leapt
out like I was on fire.

"Thanks anyway," I shouted, and slammed the door shut.

The guy yelled something, but I didn't hear what it was
because I was racing back down the street as fast as I could
to cover the hundred yards to the parking lot of the gas station. After coming all this way I really did not need to end
up being raped and kidnapped by a psycho fisherman and
left for dead on the side of some rural byway. When I got
back to the Dead River Convenience store I was wildly out
of breath. The guy behind the counter turned to look at me
as I burst through the door.

Last time I was inside I had noticed a pay phone in the
corner of the store, over by where the motor oil was stacked,
and I went right to it.

Since I began on this trip, I had imagined walking up to
my grandfather's house, across his front lawn, then knocking on the door to surprise him, but apparently that was not
to be. I was still breathing hard when I picked up the phone.

I didn't even know my grandfather's number. I hung up and grabbed the big telephone book sitting on the ledge below the phone. The number was easy enough to find—there was exactly one Harold Willows living in Bennelton, Maine. I put in the last quarter I had and waited. It rang and rang and I began to panic. My grandfather and his wife were so old they probably didn't even have voice mail. What if no one was home—what if they were away?

I let it continue to ring while I tried to figure out what to do. I was going to have to call my parents. The idea of that sucked on many, many levels.

And then someone picked up the receiver.

"Yyy-ello!" a voice shouted into my ear.

"Grandpa?" I called back.

There was a pause. "Who's this?"

"Grandpa, it's Lucy," I said. "Your granddaughter. Remember?"

There was another pause. Then his voice was so loud I had to hold the phone away from my ear.

"Of course I remember. I thought maybe you were your grandmother phoning. I ran in from outside. Hello Lu*lu*, what are you doing calling me up?"

"I'm here," I said. I was squeezing the receiver so hard my hand started to ache. "I've come to see you."

"Me? Is your father with you, and your mother and sister? Where are you guys?"

"No, it's just me. I came up on the bus."

"On the bus?"

"Yeah. Well, three buses."

"That's a hell of a trip. Where are you?"

"I'm actually in Belfast." I explained about falling asleep and missing my stop and how I was out of money and the not very nice bus driver— but not about the guy in the pickup truck. I was talking really fast; I couldn't slow down.

"Well, hold on now," my grandfather said. "You wait right there. I'll be out to get you in a jiff."

When I hung up the phone I was so relieved and excited I didn't know what to do. I walked around the aisles of the store really fast without even seeing anything. Then I was outside, over by the road, looking up and down, then back inside the store. I wanted a Reese's Cup, but I had exactly three cents to my name.

I tried to sit on the bench by the road, but either it had bad memories of the guy in the truck or I was just too excited to sit still. After about a half hour, a car pulled into the parking lot and came right over to where I was standing. As it pulled up, the passenger-side window rolled down and there was my grandpa's face, smiling out at me.

"There she is," he said, and opened the door to get out. My grandfather still moved pretty fast for such an old person. He was the spry, wiry type. He stood looking at me for a second—then he hugged me. I was kind of surprised by the hug; I don't know what I expected. It's not like he was the best hugger in the world; it was kind of a boney and hard hug, but nice nonetheless.

He turned and opened the back door for me. When I got in, I saw that there was another guy in the driver's seat. It was hard to tell exactly how old he was, but I got a feeling he might be younger than he looked. His hair was super messy and his beard was splotchy, as if it could only grow in certain areas. It made his face look like a partially mowed lawn.

"This is Davis," my grandfather said. "He rents the apartment above the garage."

Davis reached his hand over the seat. He had a really strong handshake. "Hey," he said. His voice was deep.

"Hi," I said.

"Davis works at the fish-processing plant," my grandfather said.

I didn't know what to say to that. I had no idea what they did at a fish-processing plant. Weren't fish just fish, and you ate them? What had to be processed?

"Oh," was all I could think to say. "That's cool."

"Not really," Davis said. "But it pays the rent."

"Which is all that matters," my grandfather said. Then he laughed and slapped Davis on the shoulder. Davis laughed a little too, but not as much as my grandfather. He pulled the car out onto the road and headed toward Bennelton.

"I'm not driving too much these days," my grandfather

said. "My eyes. Davis here had just gotten home from work, so he was kind enough to zip me out to get you." My grandfather was sort of half turning over his shoulder but not really looking at me.

"Thank you for coming to get me. I wanted it to be a surprise, but . . ." I shrugged.

"It certainly is a surprise," my grandfather said. "What led to this momentous decision to come up here on your own like this?"

Before I could answer, my grandfather spoke again.

"Wait, do your parents know you're here?"

"Not exactly," I said.

I didn't know what to expect at that point. I just hoped he wouldn't put me back on the bus headed south. Instead, my grandfather burst out laughing.

"I love it," he shouted. He slapped his palm against his thigh a few times. "Your father never would have done something like that in a million years. Must come from your mother's side of the family." He was still laughing.

I told him about my great-grandmother, whom I was named after, who ran away from home with a vacuum cleaner salesman.

"That must be it." Grandpa nodded his head and laughed again.

He had a good strong laugh, stronger than you might have thought if you just looked at him. I hoped to hear plenty more of it.

15

———

MY GRANDFATHER'S HOUSE was a lot like I remembered it. It had a gravel driveway shaped like a big U in front starting in one corner of the yard, swinging up to the house, and then swooping back down to the other corner of the yard, so you never had to back up to go in and out. Davis stopped at the top of the U, right in front of the door. He tossed the keys to my grandfather across the hood of the car and headed over toward his apartment above the garage.

"Good to meet you, Lucy," he said over his shoulder. "I'm sure I'll be seeing you around."

"Not if she sees you first," my grandfather called after him.

"You're welcome, old man," Davis yelled back at him without turning around. He swung open the metal screen door and I could see stairs right inside. I hadn't even noticed there was an apartment with someone living there the last time I was here.

"Angela is away in Germany visiting her sister, so it's just us," my grandfather said as he reached to open the door.

"Oh, when is she coming back?"

"Another eight days; she's been gone nearly a week."

I followed him through the small dining room where we had all split one tiny chicken when we were here. In the kitchen it was clear right away that my grandfather was home alone. Dishes were piled up in the sink. A Wheaties cereal box sat out on the counter with its top open, a carton of rice milk beside it.

The room was a typical kitchen, although very old. Over the white stove was a clock with the face of the moon painted on it. Above it, protruding from a plastic stick, a cow swung back and forth keeping the seconds. I remembered loving that clock the last time we were here. I'd forgotten it—the cow jumping over the moon, very childish; but so what, it was cool.

My grandfather looked around the room. "I was just about to have a bite to eat when you called," he said. "But now that you're here, I suppose we ought to celebrate with something a little nicer than cereal."

"Cereal is fine," I said.

"No, no. I can't tell your father that we had cereal for dinner on your first night. He already thinks little enough of me as it is."

"We don't have to tell him I'm here," I said softly.

My grandfather stopped looking around and stared at me; then he nodded. It seemed like he was nodding more to himself than to me. He walked right past me out of the kitchen and into the dining room, the way we came in.

"Coming?" he called over his shoulder.

Town was a block and a half up the hill to the left. On the corner, beneath Main Street's lone traffic light, was a family-style restaurant with large windows. It was the only place to eat except for a Chinese restaurant and a fish and chips place, which were across the street from each other down at the end of town, two blocks away. I had eaten breakfast at the family place once before. They had very good chocolate chip pancakes, so I figured their dinner would be good too.

It was. We both had the meatloaf with mashed potatoes and gravy. It was exactly what I needed. The food landed hard in my stomach and stayed there. It was just what I needed.

The restaurant had about twelve tables in the middle and four booths against the wall. We were in a booth with a green tablecloth. The only things on it were a small, unlit candle in a clear glass holder and a tiny vase with a daisy sticking out. It was still kind of early, so only two other tables had people at them. Grandpa said hello to a few folks who came in after we were seated, and introduced me as his granddaughter Lulu.

I didn't know what we were going to talk about, but actually conversation rolled quite easily. He asked me about school—but not too much.

"An' how's that sister of yours getting on?"

"She's okay," I said. "I haven't really seen her around much lately."

"Where'd she go off to?"

"No, she's around. She's doing one of her plays, as usual. I just meant . . ." I shrugged. "I don't know."

Mostly my grandfather rambled on about life in the town: the fishing boats and the lobstermen. And he talked about the bread delivery truck he used to drive for a few years until about six months ago when his eyes got too bad. He got up at three in the morning and had to go to this bakery-type warehouse to pick up bread and drive it all over the place, delivering to stores and restaurants for the morning. Apparently, he covered a lot of territory while everyone slept.

"Didn't think I would enjoy that job, driving around in the middle of the night like that. But there was something about it. Yes siree, real peaceful."

"It sounds kind of spooky. Those dark, winding roads all alone every night."

"Yeah, and what if I'd got a flat tire or something? Big Foot might have come out of the woods and eaten me." He laughed that laugh of his. The one that showed half his teeth were missing. It was a very satisfying laugh.

"Some nights Angela would come with me. I enjoyed that too, but honestly, I think I preferred it alone. Gave me time to think."

"About what?" I asked him. I was very curious what my grandfather thought about while driving around in the woods all night long, all alone.

"Life." He grinned and rubbed the palms of his hands together, like he had been hatching a master plan for the universe.

We both laughed.

When the lady cleared our plates my grandfather asked me if I wanted dessert. "They have pretty good ice cream here. Not the best, but not bad."

"Thanks, Harold," the waitress said. I wasn't sure if she was being sarcastic or not.

"Just calling 'em like I see 'em, Shirley."

"Uh-huh."

"What flavors do you have?" I asked.

"Vanilla. Chocolate. Strawberry." She was kind of a tough lady.

I ordered one scoop of chocolate and one scoop of vanilla. The waitress looked at my grandfather, and he shook his head.

"I thought you liked ice cream," I said once the waitress was gone.

"Not like—*love*," he said. "But my doctor told me I had to cut out dairy. I'm not really sure why at this point, but them's the orders."

When my ice cream arrived, the waitress had added some whipped cream and a cherry on top. I don't know if it was the cherry that did it, but as she was walking away, my grandfather called after her.

"Shirley, I'll have the same!"

I looked up with a mouthful of ice cream. "But I thought—"

"Rules are for fools," my grandfather said. "Never forget that."

I knew it was bad for him, but I was really happy that he ordered the ice cream. On the bus ride up I had been hoping we'd go back to that ice cream stand where we went the last time, so if we couldn't do that, I at least wanted to share some ice cream somewhere.

My grandfather watched while I ate half my bowl, until his arrived. We didn't speak while we ate. When he was finished, my grandfather wiped his mouth with a napkin. "De-li-cious," he said, as if it was three words. He had missed a spot with his napkin, just like he did that last time, but I didn't say anything.

When we left the restaurant, the traffic signal was blinking red in one direction and yellow in the other. Quiet was not the word for this place—more like silent. We walked home, my grandfather chatting happily the whole way with a smudge of chocolate on his face.

It seemed my visit had perked Grandpa up a bit. As I was getting ready for bed, he was whistling and doing that huge pile of dishes that had clearly been gathering in the sink all week.

My room had a big, old wooden sleigh bed in it with a bunch of old quilts on top, even though it was not cold at all. As I was falling asleep, which was happening a lot faster than I thought it would in a strange place, I started to hear thunder. I'm generally not a huge fan of thunder and lightning. I once heard about a guy who was hit by lightning and lived but then couldn't ever remember anything new that happened to him afterward. He remembered things that had happened twenty years earlier, but he had no idea what he ate for breakfast that morning.

Given the weight of some of the things that had been looping around in my mind over the past few months, starting every day over with only happy old memories didn't sound like such a bad way to go through life. In any case, I felt quite safe and sound under all those quilts and covers. It seemed not much could trouble my mind here in Maine.

When I awoke in the morning, the sun was shining and birds were singing, literally. Birds were right outside my window. When I looked out I could see a bright red cardinal singing his lungs out on a branch five feet from the glass.

I slipped into the bathroom and had a quick shower, which felt awfully nice after such a trip. There was a huge crack in the shower wall. It was taped over but didn't seem like it would hold for long, so I tried not to splash it too much.

I jumped into the same clothes I had been wearing since I left home almost two days earlier—even this did not dampen my mood. The only thing I missed was Simon. As I made my way down the creaky stairs, I was thinking that he and Grandpa would like each other a lot. They both had that slightly devilish sense of humor that I liked so much.

"Good morning, Lulu," Grandpa called as he heard me coming a few steps before I hit the kitchen. You certainly could not sneak up on anybody in this house to commit a murder—everywhere you went, the floor announced your arrival.

"Morning, Grandpa." The kitchen smelled like cinnamon. "Is that French toast?"

"Your favorite, I believe." He had on an apron that said *Queen of the Kitchen* across the chest, with a big crown sitting on top of the Q.

I leaned up against the countertop beside the stove where he had two thick pieces of bread turning golden brown in a frying pan, creating that succulent aroma.

"Is that Grandma's apron?"

"What gave you that idea?" He was concentrating pretty hard on the French toast. His tongue was curled up on his lip in exactly the way I had noticed Thomas doing when he was cruising on his skateboard.

"Grab the syrup in the door of the fridge," Grandpa said as he dished up breakfast. I took a seat beside him at the table and looked out the window over the front lawn, which needed mowing, as I chewed.

"How did you know French toast was my favorite thing for breakfast?"

"I asked your mother when I talked to your parents last night." My grandfather looked up at me with a big piece of French toast puffing up the left side of his mouth, the side with teeth where he could chew. "I figured they might have been concerned," he said through the food.

"What did they say?"

"They were very relieved to know you were safe," he said, still chewing as if this conversation meant nothing at all.

"I sent them an email," I said quietly.

"And they were very glad to get that. They had just called the police."

"I was afraid of that." It was hard to believe that I had been gone less than two days.

My grandfather took another big bite of his breakfast. "I told them we had meatloaf and mashed potatoes for dinner, and I asked what your favorite thing for breakfast was."

"Oh."

"They also wanted to know if I was sure it was you since they had never known you to eat meatloaf before."

"I eat it at school sometimes," I mumbled. I was staring down into my plate. "They don't know everything there is to know about me."

"Your father was going to come up today and get you—"

"Oh, no—"

"—but I asked him to give us a couple of days. I was just getting to know my granddaughter, I told him."

"What did he say to that?"

"He said he'd call tonight, and we'd see."

"That sounds like him."

"Yes, it does, doesn't it?" Grandpa got up for more coffee.

When he had finished refilling his cup he came back and sat down again. I could smell his coffee breath from across the table. My American History teacher had the worst coffee breath on the planet. I think it's what made me dislike history class so much. But since this coffee was still pretty fresh, and since I liked my grandfather a great deal, I didn't mind it at all. It smelled kind of exotic. Why is it that the same thing that can drive you crazy or disgust you about one person can seem really interesting or worldly in another?

"So you ever going to tell me what brought you all the way up here all by your lonesome, causing your parents all sorts of panic?"

Part of me wanted to tell him about Thomas, but

another part felt I shouldn't. I suppose I felt ashamed. I wasn't the one who had done something wrong, but still, I just couldn't say anything—at this point anyway.

"I don't know." I shrugged. "Just needed a break, I guess."

My grandfather looked at me for a good long while. Then he nodded his head. "Oh, I think I can understand that."

16

MY GRANDFATHER AND I cleaned out the gutters. Actually, I held the ladder while he climbed up and pulled out dead leaves and all sorts of gunk from the metal drains that clung to the edge of the roof. I had to do this once at home with my father, but for some reason it didn't bother me as much in Maine.

"Look out below," my grandfather called every time he was about to drop another handful of mucky glop he'd dug out from those disgusting things. He was seeing how close he could get it to me without hitting me. It was actually pretty funny. One time he misjudged, and it went all over my shirt.

"Hey!" I screamed at him, laughing. "Watch out or I'll tip this ladder over."

He laughed, too. "Well, that shirt was so dirty already I can hardly see the difference."

When we had finished the gutters along the front of the house he climbed down. We raked the little globs into several piles and then my grandfather threw down the rake, tossed back his shoulders, and shouted, "Lunch!" As he opened the screen door he glanced over his shoulder at me. "We'll do the back tomorrow."

Once inside, he went upstairs and came down with a T-shirt that must have belonged to Angela. It was more of an old-person T-shirt than a regular T-shirt, if you know what I mean. But it wasn't bad; it was black with a sparkling picture of the Eiffel Tower on it.

"At least it's clean." Grandpa smiled as he tossed it to me. It even kind of fit.

There wasn't a lot in the fridge, but we found enough for grilled cheese. When we were finished, Grandpa pushed his chair back. "Now," he said, "nap, then bowling."

I wasn't in much of a napping mood, since I had slept so well the night before, so while Grandpa slept I wandered from room to room. The place definitely had an old-person smell about it, which I was actually enjoying. On the bookshelf in the den I found an old high school yearbook that belonged to my dad. I couldn't believe it. Last year when I got my high school yearbook for the first time, my dad had tried to find his senior yearbook and couldn't—here it was.

I hated to admit it, but his page was actually pretty cute. There were two photos on it. In one his hair was long, and he was looking just past the camera. It was a pretty stiff, formal shot. But in the other photo he was with a friend, and they were both smiling directly at the camera—they looked so young and happy. I don't think I've ever seen my dad look so carefree.

There was also a quote on the page. Most of the kids had quotes from rock songs on their pages, but my dad had lines from a poem by Robert Frost. ". . . I have promises to keep, and miles to go before I sleep, and miles to go before I sleep." It seemed fitting for my dad. Responsible.

I was about to flip the page when I noticed something down on the bottom right corner, tucked away, as if it was hiding there, clinging to the edge of the book. It was another quote—"But if dreams came true, oh, wouldn't that be nice." Beneath it, the quote was attributed to *B. Springsteen*, who I knew my dad liked from his classic rock radio station, so it was no accident that it was there. If dreams came true, oh, wouldn't that be nice? So true, but so unlike my dad. So wistful. I stared and stared at that quote.

Eventually my grandfather came downstairs singing some song about it being a long way to Tipperary, wherever that is.

"Let's go, Lulu," he called out.

I shoved the yearbook back on the shelf and chased after him out the door. Davis was already waiting by my grandfather's car.

"Friday is bowling day," Grandpa said as we piled in. The bowling alley was a few miles out of town down the main road in a low white building with a red roof, standing by itself in a parking lot. It actually looked like a very, very long trailer home, with that kind of metal siding that looks sort of temporary, but isn't.

There were more lanes inside than I thought there could be, about twenty or so. The ceiling was low, the place was pretty cluttered. Trophies were sitting haphazardly up on shelves, a banner on the wall proclaimed *Mid-Coast Regional Finals 4th Place 1998*, an old pinball machine with a mermaid theme had been shoved into a corner, and of course there was a big rack of really used-looking bowling shoes for rent. It was an old movie come to life.

But what was really bizarre was that the bowling was something called candlepin bowling, which is totally different from regular bowling. Not that I'm a big bowler—in fact, I've done it maybe a dozen times in my entire life—but I had never heard of this before. The ball was much smaller and the pins were tall and skinny.

"That's the way we do it up here in God's country," my grandfather said.

"I think it came from Canada," Davis said as he was leaning over tying his shoes.

I liked it a lot better than regular bowling. First, you got three chances each time instead of two, and since the ball was so much smaller I didn't have to twist out of the way or smash it into my thigh like I always did with regular bowling. I almost broke 100 in the first game, which would have been a personal best.

The place was so old, they didn't have electronic scoreboards. My grandfather showed me how to keep score with a paper and pencil.

"Your father loved to keep score," he told me.

"Dad used to bowl?"

"Are you kidding me? Your father was a superb bowler."

"No way."

"I swear to you."

"Weird," I said.

"Had his own bowling ball too. Wasn't a candlepin ball, but he had a purple bowling ball."

"*Purple?*"

"With his name engraved on it."

"You're making this up."

"*Mike*, it said."

"*Mike?*" I screamed. "You're totally making this up!"

"I swear on my life," my grandfather said and made some weird crossing sign in front of himself. "Not only that, but he was in a junior league for a few years. I think he was team captain one season."

"Captain? Did they wear those ridiculous shirts?"

"I think they just had T-shirts, if memory serves me correct, which it does less and less these days." He laughed. "Then he just grew out of it, or lost interest. One day it was done. That's the way it was with your father. When he was done he was done."

My grandfather was quiet for a while. "Don't know what the hell ever happened to that ball," he said softly.

"I can't believe this, that's crazy," I said. "When he's taken us a few times, or I've had to go bowling for some stupid birthday party, he has never mentioned he was on a bowling team."

For dinner we drove a few miles into Rockport, which was a much nicer town than Bennelton.

"You ever eat sushi?" my grandfather asked. The three of us were walking past some fairly fancy shops on the very quaint Main Street.

"My fave," I said.

"I knew I liked you for a reason," Grandpa said.

"You buying, old man?" Davis asked.

My grandfather gave him a quick look out of the corner of his eye that I'm not sure he knew I saw. Davis smiled.

The sushi place had a small Japanese flag hanging outside. Inside, big white ball-shaped paper lamps dangled from the ceiling. It was very Zen. I liked it right away.

"You eat sushi often, Lucy?" Davis asked me as the waiter brought us hot towels to clean our hands. "I don't think I ate sushi till a few years ago."

"My granddaughter is very sophisticated," Grandpa said as he scrubbed his face with his towel.

"Unlike her grandfather," Davis said.

"Very true." Grandpa grinned his half-toothless grin and tossed his towel back on the little canoe-shaped woven tray.

"It's my father's favorite thing to eat," I told Davis, "so we get it pretty often."

"Really?" Grandpa said. "I wouldn't think he'd be so adventurous. Good for him."

"Well," I said, "he does order the same thing every time."

For some reason my grandfather thought that was the funniest thing he had ever heard. He laughed so hard that people started to look around from nearby tables.

After dinner we had some mint leaf ice cream, which I had never heard of before, but was super delicious. The only person I have ever met who eats ice cream faster than me is my grandfather. Since I still had no clothes except what I came in and the borrowed Eiffel Tower shirt, my grandfather bought me a very cool T-shirt with crazy Japanese writing on it.

Back home, the phone was ringing as we walked through the door.

"Yello!" my grandfather shouted into the receiver. After a brief pause he said, "Hello, Michael. How are you?"

He listened for a bit more, all the while looking right at me.

"We're doing great. Aren't we, Lulu? Would you like to speak with her?"

He held out the receiver. I took it from him.

"Hi, Dad," I said.

"Well, there you are," my father said. His tone was really flat, like he was trying to be very normal.

"Yup, I'm right here," I said.

"Are you all right?"

"Yeah, I'm great. We just had sushi." I was trying to sound very upbeat.

"Uh-huh." He couldn't have cared less. "What was the idea of this stunt, Lucy? Your mother has been worried sick. So have I."

"I'm sorry, I—"

"We'll talk about it when I come and get you." He cut me off hard. "I have several open houses this weekend, but I'm planning to come up on Monday, as long as everything there is still okay."

"Things are great here."

"Uh-huh," he said again. "Your mother wants to speak with you. Hold on."

"Okay."

"Hold on," he repeated. Where exactly did he think I was going at this point?

My mom was a bit gentler, asking how I was getting on

and what we were doing. She was glad I was eating so well. But she didn't totally give me a pass.

"Your father and I are very, very upset, Lucy. Anything could have happened to you." I explained to her that my father didn't need to come up and get me. I was totally fine, and I could take the bus back down in a few days.

"I know your father wants to go up to get you, but there is a lot going on at work, so we'll see," my mother said. "Hang on, your father wants to speak with you again."

My dad must have been standing right next to my mom.

"Lucy?"

"Yes."

I could tell something was coming.

"What could you have possibly been thinking, going over to Thomas's house like that?"

I wanted to scream, "What the hell did you expect me to do once I found out that I had a brother living a few blocks away? Just be a loser and ignore it, like you?"

I didn't say anything.

I didn't sleep as well that night as I had the night before—not after that call.

I woke up just as it was getting light. Grandpa's house was quiet, but a different quiet than my own house. I lay in bed for a long time. I really didn't know what I was going to do about anything.

I had closed the window before going to sleep since it was still chilly up here in the north at night, and so I got up to open it. The birds were singing again as I got back into bed. I remembered the cardinal and thought about getting back up to see if he was the one singing. Instead I tucked in deeper under the covers. After a little while I thought I could hear people talking outside. Then I definitely heard my grandfather's laugh, so I got up and went to the window.

Grandpa was by the edge of his property, talking over the shrubs with the woman next door. She was tending her garden, planting something. Their conversation drifted up to me.

". . . he never knew we knew." My grandfather was in the middle of a story, waving his hands around. "It was his mother who finally solved the mystery. She found out that the girl loved tomatoes."

The woman laughed. "How?"

"We had a Fourth of July block party, and our cute little blond neighbor had her paper plate piled high with slices of only juicy red tomatoes."

The woman laughed again. "You are a stitch, Harold," she said to him. I'd never heard anyone call someone a stitch before. My grandfather laughed.

"It was like clockwork," he went on. "Every time I'd pick one and put it on the windowsill to ripen, the next day it would be gone. We never suspected it might be Michael, since when we asked him about it he looked so confused and shook his head. He was normally such an honest kid."

"Honest, really? You sure he was your son?" They both

laughed again. They were having a high old time at the crack of dawn.

"Broke his teenage heart when they moved away. His daughter Lucy is up with me now, visiting for a while." He sort of turned to gesture toward the house and I dove back from the window. I didn't want him to see me eavesdropping.

While I was taking a shower and trying not to get water all over the giant taped-up crack, I couldn't get out of my head the fact that my father had been in love with a tomato-eating blond when he was a thieving teenage bowler who had harbored secret dreams. Would I ever be able to look at a tomato the same way again? Or a bowling ball? Or even listen to *B. Springsteen* for that matter?

17

———

GRANDPA AND I DID THE GUTTERS on the back of the house after breakfast. It wasn't as much fun as the day before. We left the lumps of glop on the ground where they lay. We didn't even rake them into piles this time.

"Do you know where I can send an email?" I asked my grandfather as he was putting the ladder back in the garage.

"There's the library just out of town or there's a coffee shop down by the pier that has a couple of computers you can rent for a half hour at a time," he said. "That's where I usually go, not that I send too many emails."

We headed down the hill toward the water. There was no sidewalk so we walked along the edge of the road.

Evergreen trees lined the street, so not much light got through, even though it was a sunny day. There was hardly any breeze, either. We were quiet as we walked, and I listened to our feet slapping the pavement.

The water was three blocks away The harbor wasn't one of those picture-postcard places you might think it would be, with charming boats bobbing in a happy sea. This one was kind of scraggly, even in the bright light. There was a muddy beach, which my grandfather said was only that way because the tide was out and that it was under water most of the time. A few small sailboats sat on the mud, tipped over a little bit on their sides, like bathtub toys nobody put away after the plug was pulled. A small house stood at the end of a long wooden pier. Nobody lived in it, obviously, but I wasn't sure what it was for. Maybe it was the fish-processing place where Davis worked. I didn't ask. Other boats farther out in the harbor were all pretty small, and most needed a coat of paint. A giant rusted motor lay off to one side. I didn't ask what that had been used for either. I didn't feel like asking a lot of questions. With the excitement of arriving, and hanging out with my grandfather, and just the way life was up here, I hadn't worried about much of anything at all, but since my father's call, everything had come rushing back.

"That's it right over there, where you can send an email." My grandfather pointed to a place called The Last Drop. "Come on, I could use a coffee anyway."

"Hello there, Harold," the older woman behind the counter called out as we entered the small store. She had short gray hair and large glasses.

"Hello, Eunice," he called back. "This is my granddaughter Lulu."

"Lulu? That's an unusual name," she said.

"Oh, cut it out. Her name is Lucy," Grandpa said.

"Well, how am I supposed to know that when you introduce her as Lulu?"

"Because no one is named Lulu; it's a nickname, for God's sake."

Eunice shook her head. They both appeared to enjoy the bickering. My grandfather seemed well liked in these parts.

Eunice finally turned to me. "Well hello, Lucy."

My grandfather ordered himself a coffee and a Coke for me, and Eunice gave me a slip of paper with the Internet login on it. The computers were in the back of the room, on a long table facing the wall. Grandpa took a seat by the window and sipped his coffee while I went to work.

I'M SORRY, I wrote. *I don't know what's wrong with me except that I'm a total idiot. You are the greatest person I have ever met on the planet and I just flipped out. This whole Thomas situation has made me nuts, even if it doesn't always seem that way. Please please forgive me, Simon. I ran away up to Maine to see my grandfather, who you would actually like a lot. I'll be back next week, I think. I will call you then (I left my phone at home) and hopefully you will still want to talk to me.* Then I wrote, *If you don't I don't know what I will do,* but I deleted it because it sounded way too lame and desperate. I signed it, *LOVE, ME*

Once that was done I felt a lot better. I wished there was something I could have done about Thomas to feel better too. I wished I could have written him an email and made him just disappear. At this point I would have settled for just rewinding the whole night on the back deck and never even knowing about him.

Outside, a man was sitting on the edge of the pier mending a lobster trap on his lap. His feet were dangling over the edge. Beside him was a massive pile of traps. If he had to fix each and every one of those, he was in for a very long day.

The coolest thing about the whole waterside was the lighthouse a little off to the left, at the end of a wall of giant stones. My grandfather said it was man-made.

"How did they do that? Isn't it deep?" I asked him.

"Big cranes, bulldozers. I saw them repairing it last year."

"How far is it to the lighthouse?"

"Want to go?"

He could see the look on my face. He laughed.

"It's a half mile out, over some pretty uneven stones. If you're up for it . . ."

"No problem," I said. I needed to clear my head anyway.

The boulders that made the breakwater were unevenly spaced. It was fairly level, but some of the gaps were treacherous. You had to constantly look down at where you were walking. The wind was blowing nice and warm once we got away from land, the sun was reflecting off the water, and the boats out sailing around this way and that.

"Do you know how to sail, Grandpa?"

"I wish I did, Lulu."

"Me, too."

We had been picking our way out toward the lighthouse for about fifteen minutes when I asked my grandfather something I'd been thinking about before I got to Maine. With everything else going on since I got here, I'd forgotten it—until my father called.

"Grandpa?" I said.

"Yes, Lulu."

"How come you don't like my father?"

My grandfather stopped walking. That made me stop, too. He looked at me for what felt like a long time. Then he nodded slowly, in that way I'd seen him do a few times already, as if he was answering a question that only he could hear in his mind—not necessarily the question you had asked him.

"Is that what he said to you?"

"Well, he didn't say it to me exactly, but I heard him say it."

A sailboat was cruising past very close to where we were standing. The people on board were laughing, holding drinks, their hair blowing in the breeze, as if they really didn't have a care. I wondered if I'd die without ever having been to sea.

Finally Grandpa started walking out toward the lighthouse again.

"Did you know that when I was a kid my father owned a candy store?" he said.

"Really?"

He shrugged. "It wasn't as great as everyone thought it was. It's not like he owned a candy store or anything."

"Wait, you just said—"

"I know. What I'm saying is that we think we know what something is like, or would be like, or we think we know someone, but we don't ever really know, unless we live it ourselves. That's all. Mostly what I remember about growing up was not the free candy, but my father sitting on the couch drinking two six-packs of beer and passing out every night. And it's not that it even seemed bad. It was just the way things were. We see things the way we see them. But other people might see the same things a different way."

I felt really bad for my grandfather, but he kept walking that jaunty walk he had, like a little terrier scampering over the rocks. Then he pointed toward the rocks a few feet in front of us.

"You see that crab there?"

"Where?" I screamed.

He laughed. It was good to hear that laugh again, but I was not happy to hear about crabs.

"He's just living his crab life, he's not meaning you any harm, but you have this reaction to him, like he's going to get you. He's just trying to not get eaten by some seagull, that's all.

"Now, you say your father believes I didn't like him. That saddens me, of course, but he can never know what I felt, what I experienced. Look, we never see our parents as just people. They are our parents, and that ought to be enough for them, but I'll let you in on a little secret, Lulu—it's not enough."

I could now see all sorts of tiny crab-type shelled thingies scampering between the stones and all over the place.

"Your father, he's a pretty responsible guy."

"Well, you don't know him very well," I said.

"You're right," he said. "I don't. And it's a goddamn shame."

"He seems all responsible," I said, "but you don't know everything about a person like you think you do."

"That's just what I've been saying," my grandfather said.

But he had no way of knowing I was talking about Thomas.

"My dad said you got mad a lot, all the time."

My grandfather just kept his eyes on the stones beneath us, picking his way out toward the lighthouse, which finally seemed to be getting closer. When he spoke again, his voice was so soft that I had to lean in closer to hear him through the wind. He told me about how he had been really in love with his wife when they were young.

"She was the most exciting person I had ever met," he said. "She made me feel the way I wanted to feel about myself. And for some reason that I'll never understand, I did the same for her." He was almost smiling at the memory of it, I could tell, but he didn't allow it to show.

"Then after a while we couldn't seem to get along in the same way. Nothing had really happened that I could see, but somehow everything started to lead to a fight." He looked out over the water.

"It must have been all my fault, especially since she never fought with anybody else, and I fought with everyone." He laughed a little at that and kept walking.

"Then she had the idea that a baby would bring us closer. We know better about that kind of thing now, but back then, that's what people thought."

We were moving quickly over the rocks at this point.

"Your father didn't sleep well as a child. He got sick a lot—whooping cough and pneumonia, all sorts of things. I was either working all the time or trying to find work. I don't know which one was worse."

I was looking over at him as he spoke—at least, I was as

much as I could, considering I had to keep lookout for the huge crevices between the rocks.

"I just think at some point she kind of gave up on me. Which, looking back on it, I can't really blame her. And she just put all the love she used to have for me onto her baby." He shrugged. "It was easier, believe me."

He was saying these things as if he was talking about going to the grocery store or something—as if it didn't have much import. The only thing that gave him away was how softly he was talking. In the brief time I had known my grandfather, *soft-spoken* was not a word that I would have used in referring to him. Then he whispered something, but I wasn't sure I heard correctly.

"What, Grandpa?" I said to him.

"I said I was jealous." His voice rang out over the sea on the breeze. "Plain and simple." He turned to me. "Crazy, huh? For a grown-up to be jealous of a little kid."

"Not so crazy, I guess."

He smiled. I think he appreciated that I said that. He went on to say that he knew his wife was busy with the new baby and had to take care of him and that she didn't really have time for my grandfather anymore and all that normal stuff—but it was something else, something more. He felt that the baby had taken his wife's love from him.

"It doesn't speak very well of me, I know," he said.

Then he stopped walking; his feet were balanced between two large rocks, and he looked at me.

"But of course, I loved your father very much. Very much. He was our only child."

He held my look for a long time. Then he started walking again. I loved my grandfather a lot right then.

"But it is true that I kicked the dog fairly often," he said.

"What does that mean?"

"It means that I had a temper when I was younger. Which I still do at times. When your father was a little kid he was easy to take things out on. Since he was young and couldn't fight back, and his mother always took his side of things, and I suppose that made me even angrier."

We were getting close to the lighthouse. "Almost there." My grandfather read my mind. Then he smiled that smile that lets you see he only has teeth on the left side of his mouth.

"What happened to your teeth, Grandpa?" I asked without thinking.

He threw back his head and laughed, really hard. I thought he might give himself whiplash or something.

"I didn't brush. So let that be a lesson to you." He wagged his finger at me. "No, actually, I got in a fight and this guy punched me and knocked out a few. He was a southpaw, caught me off guard. Once those teeth were gone, the ones in the area seemed to miss them and fell out, too, in solidarity. That was a long time ago. I just never got them fixed, which, I have to admit, was not very smart. I think I figured I was just going to get in another fight, so what was the point?"

"Did you?"

"Did I what?"

"Get in another fight?"

Grandpa smiled that toothless grin. "Lots of 'em," he said. I was getting used to that smile.

The lighthouse was behind a fence, and the gate was locked. It seemed unfair after our long walk. But there was not a soul besides us out there, and there was nothing we could do about it. After shaking the big lock a few times, we turned and started back.

The wind was blowing pretty hard this far out into the water, but it felt good against my face. As we started walking, my grandfather began to slow down. It looked as if he was picking his way along the breakwater, so that he wouldn't trip or slip between the irregularly spaced rocks. He had zipped out to the end so briskly, it had been all I could do to keep up with him, so these slow, methodical movements seemed weird. As we kept walking, he started pushing out his chest, or maybe he was arching his back. It looked strange, like an old man pretending to be a soldier or something. Then he fell backwards.

Sometimes when accidents happen everything goes in slow motion and you just watch it. Not this time. We were walking, his back was arching, and then he was down. I heard his head smack on the rocks, hard. He grunted. I heard myself gasp. He must have lost consciousness for a second or two, but then he shook himself and grabbed the back of his head. He looked around as if he didn't know how he had gotten on the ground.

"Help me up, Lucy," he said.

It was the first time he had called me by my real name the whole trip.

"Maybe you ought to just sit there a second, Grandpa," I said, crouching by his side. I was breathing hard.

"No, I'm fine," he said, trying to push himself up.

Once he was sitting he stopped moving, as if rushing to get up was not such a good idea.

"I must have slipped on the wet rocks," he said.

The section of the breakwater we had been walking over was dry. In fact, the whole thing was surprisingly absent of seawater.

"Yeah," I said to him, and put my hand on his shoulder. The fall was scary, but till that moment I'd been telling myself that old people fall down, right? Then this made me think that perhaps something more serious than him just losing his balance was going on. I plopped down next to him. Seagulls flew overhead, squawking at us. The wind was still blowing hard, lifting my grandfather's thin hair. We sat there on the rocks with our breath going in and out, the both of us.

Eventually my grandfather rolled over onto one hip and started to push himself up. I helped him till we both were standing.

"Let's go," he said. He was trying to sound confident, but his voice was shaky.

"You sure?" I asked.

"Let's move," he snapped. It was the first time I ever saw a flash of his anger.

We stared toward the land, which looked very far off. Right away I could see that he was still arching and leaning back. I put my arm around his waist. I thought he'd yell at me not to, but he didn't say anything. What would my dad do? I slowed down our pace.

As he started to arch back farther, I slid my arm between his shoulder blades, as if to prop him up, but there was no way that I was going to be able to keep him vertical if he continued to push back as strongly as he was.

"Are you okay, Grandpa?"

"Fine, Lulu," he said. I was Lulu again. "Just slippery back there." He didn't seem aware at all that he was pressing back into my arm. We were walking forward, but it was as if he was pushing back against our progress at the same time. I wished Simon were there.

Then my grandfather fell back like a tree. Since I was trying to hold him up, I went down with him. My arm was beneath him as we hit. I smacked my elbow. His body hit hard.

"Shit," my grandfather said, trying to roll over as soon as we hit the stones. There was panic in his movement. Pain was shooting down my arm.

Once we were both sitting, we didn't make much more

of an effort to move. I was rubbing my elbow; my grandfather stared straight ahead.

"You okay, Grandpa?"

He nodded. He was definitely more than just shaky now.

"Did you hurt yourself?" he managed to ask, without looking at me.

"No, I'm tip-top," I said.

I saw a man and a boy walking out along the breakwater in our direction. They were far away, still pretty close to land, carrying what seemed to be fishing rods.

"Grandpa," I said, "I'm going to run up and get some help. I want you to stay right here and not move till I get back. Okay?"

I expected him to tell me that I was going to do no such thing. He didn't. He simply nodded and said, "All right."

I bolted down that breakwater. Because of the crazy way the rocks were spaced out, my strides were really uneven. I almost went down several times, but didn't slow my pace.

This was my fault—if we hadn't been out there, it wouldn't have happened. If I hadn't pushed Grandpa about my father, he wouldn't have gotten upset and fallen. If I hadn't flipped out about Thomas in the first place, I wouldn't have taken off from home and come up here and caused all this trouble.

When I was about fifty yards from the man and kid I called out.

"Help," I yelled. "I need some help!"

They looked up right away. After a second the father laid down his fishing rod and started toward me.

"My grandfather fell back there and we need help," I shouted as I came up to them.

"Do you need an ambulance?" the man asked. He was very calm.

"I think so, yes," I said. I could hear myself panting hard.

"Okay." He pulled out his phone. "Oliver, you run back and wait by the shore for the ambulance."

The kid took off without a word.

"Show me," the man said.

We didn't run, but we moved very quickly. He called 911 as we went and told them we needed an ambulance and where we were. His voice was very clear and he was super deliberate in the way he spoke.

"What happened?" he asked me when he hung up.

I explained as best I could and he kept nodding his head as we walked. When we got to my grandfather, he was still sitting on the rocks. He didn't look any worse than when I left him, but he didn't look too sure of anything anymore either.

"Who's this?" he said as the man and I arrived.

"Hi there. I'm Edward," the man said. "Can I give you a hand?"

"If you want to," my grandfather said. Then he tried to push himself up.

"You sure you want to stand up?" Edward asked.

"Of course I'm sure," my grandfather said.

Edward reached out his hand. "Maybe we should just sit tight for a few minutes."

"Maybe you should mind your own business," Grandpa snapped at him.

"Grandpa, this man is just trying to help us," I said softly.

The wind picked up for a few seconds and everyone's hair was blowing.

"All right, all right," my grandfather said, and tried to push himself up again. "But I'm fine."

Edward went around behind my grandfather and put his hands under Grandpa's armpits and hoisted him to his feet.

"How's that?" Edward asked. "Okay?"

"Why wouldn't it be?" Grandpa seemed to have no idea that at this point he looked like a windup toy soldier gone wrong.

We started walking back toward land. I was on one side and Edward was on the other, each of us with an arm around my grandfather's back. Right away Grandpa began arching again, leaning back hard. If Edward hadn't been there, nothing I could have done would have kept Grandpa on his feet. Then my grandfather's knees started to lock and he began walking stiff legged.

Out of the blue, my grandfather began asking Edward all sorts of questions: Where was he from? What did he do for a living? What kind of car did he drive? If you didn't know what was happening and only heard a recording of the conversation, you might have thought they were having a friendly chat on the street corner, or over coffee.

Up on land, the ambulance arrived. Edward must have seen it too, because he slowed and we lowered my grandfather to the ground to wait for the paramedics to come out to us.

When they arrived, they asked my grandfather how he was feeling. "Great," he said.

"What happened?" the taller paramedic asked.

"I don't know. I must have slipped back there on the wet stones."

My grandfather said he didn't want to go to the hospital and insisted that he was fine. Once the paramedics got him to his feet and explained that he was doing this strange backward-leaning thing, he looked confused. He turned to me. I shrugged. I hated betraying him.

"I think the hospital is a good idea, Grandpa," I said finally.

18

I'D NEVER RIDDEN in an ambulance before, and if you want to know the truth, I don't ever need to again. At the hospital, they placed my grandfather in a small room with a curtain surrounding the bed, even though there was no other bed in the room. He seemed to relax a bit, and then within an hour it was basically as if nothing had happened.

My grandfather had apparently suffered something called a TIA, a transient ischemic attack—kind of a "mini-stroke." The doctor at the tiny medical center where they had taken us reminded me of the young guy who had X-rayed my ankle. He was very sincere; he looked directly into my eyes whenever he spoke to me. They couldn't be sure it was this ministroke thing, he said, but all signs pointed that way. They decided to keep my grandfather overnight for observation. Grandpa gave me a number and I called Davis to come and get me.

"He's had two TIAs before," Davis told them when he arrived.

The doctor and nurses nodded their heads and seemed pleased with themselves over this latest news.

"Unconfirmed," my grandfather barked from his hospital bed. "Unconfirmed." We were all standing around him staring down, like he was a fish in a bowl.

"It's okay, Grandpa," I said to him. "They're here to help you."

"Don't believe it," my grandfather said. He was definitely getting grumpier.

Later, after he came back from some other test, when I went to say goodbye, I swung the curtain open and he popped up like a jack-in-the-box. He had his big half-toothless grin back on his face, like a crazy carved pumpkin. I almost burst into tears when I saw him smile like that. I hugged him around the neck and told him I'd see him the next day.

Davis and I didn't speak in the car. The house felt super quiet. When I walked into the kitchen, I realized I was about to pass out from hunger. We'd been at the hospital for hours, and it was past dinnertime.

"I'll order a pizza, okay?" Davis said.

Davis said he had some things to do, so he went back to his room above the garage while we waited for the food. I sat on the front steps so I didn't have to be in the house alone.

The pizza delivery guy was young, with a lot of acne. He was kind of awkward, but his pizza was super cheesy with a nice spicy sauce. Delish. I felt a lot better as I ate. Davis said he had to work in the morning but would take me to the medical center when he got off after lunch and we'd bring Grandpa home.

After I tossed the last crust into the box, I wanted nothing more than to just head upstairs. I wasn't tired at all but it was dark, and enough was enough for one day. If I got into bed, then nothing else could happen. But first there was one more thing that had to be done.

I was surprised that my parents hadn't called, but there was no blinking light on Grandpa's answering machine when I picked up the phone to call my house back in New Jersey.

My mother answered. "How's everything there today?" she asked. Her voice was calm, so I couldn't really tell how mad she was at me at this point.

I didn't especially want to launch right in with the bad news, but I figured if I waited, when I finally did tell them, they would wonder why I had been holding back.

"Oh, my God, Lucy. Is he okay? Are you okay, sweet-heart?" All of a sudden, my mother was a super sweet, lov-ing, concerned parent again.

My father was not so gentle. It's not that he sounded angry at me so much as he was trying to get a handle on what was going on. I described twice what had happened and what the doctor had said. Then I told him that Davis had driven me home. Then I had to explain who Davis was. I could hear my father breathing hard on the phone.

"Who is at the house with you now?"

"No one. Davis is in his apartment over the garage, but that's all."

The only thing he said was my name—"Lucy"—but I could tell he was now extremely stressed.

"Dad," I said, trying to sound very nonchalant, "I'm to-tally fine." I think that made it even worse.

Now my father had made me nervous about being in the house alone—and about Davis. Davis hadn't seemed like a psycho rapist or murderer, but now I wasn't so sure. After my father said they'd call in the morning and we hung up, I locked the front door, went upstairs, and climbed into bed. I didn't think I would get any sleep, but I must have passed out in self-defense. The next thing I knew it was another bright morning, and the birds were singing again. I wondered about that cardinal, if he was out there again, if that was his spot. Did birds even have spots?

While I was considering this, I heard someone moving

around downstairs. That must have been what had woken me. I figured it was Davis; he must have had a key. If it had still been dark I would have assumed he had come to kill me, but if he hadn't done it during the night, it didn't make much sense that he'd decide to attack in the cold light of day.

Then I heard footsteps on the creaky stairs. I sat up fast and looked around for something to defend myself with. An old telescope stood on a tripod by the window. It was better than nothing. I leapt up and grabbed it.

The footsteps outside my room were coming closer. The bedroom door began to slowly swing open, creaking as it went. I pulled back the telescope and was about to throw it full force at Davis's head when my dad stepped in from the hallway.

"Lucy," he said.

"Dad!" I nearly dropped the telescope. "You scared me to death."

My father walked across the room, took the telescope out of my hands, and set it back on its tripod. He just looked at me.

"Are you all right? What are you doing?"

"I'm totally fine. You just freaked me out, sneaking up on me like that."

"I didn't sneak up on you. I drove all night to get up here."

My dad had apparently hung up the phone last night and then gotten in his car and drove eight hours while

I was asleep, just to see if I was still alive. I suppose that should have touched me. Now that I got a good look at him, he did look pretty tired. We went down to the kitchen where he started to make coffee.

"How did you get in?" I asked him after I had taken a seat on one of the counter stools.

"The back door was open."

"Yeah," I said. "I left that open on purpose. I figured something like this might happen." Granted, I might have been killed by some psycho pervert strolling by the house overnight, but I didn't want my father to take any satisfaction in the fact that I forgot to lock up, confirming his belief that I couldn't deal with the situation properly.

We heard the screen door slam and there was Davis. My dad introduced himself, thanked Davis, and got the name of the medical center where my grandfather was. Davis looked like he had slept in a tree, as usual. His hair was all over the place and he still hadn't shaved, but he acted like he was dressed in a tuxedo, all calm and confident. I felt ashamed that I had suspected him of being capable of rape and murder. But I wouldn't have thought of it if my dad hadn't planted the seed in my mind.

I was suddenly furious that my father was even there.

"You know, I'm not some little kid who needs rescuing," I told him once Davis had left. "I mean, I made it all the way to Maine without any help from anyone. I don't need to be treated like I have no abilities. I'm quite capable of taking care of myself."

My father just looked at me. "I can see that," he said.

"Are you staying long?" I asked him.

"No. *We're* not," he said. "We're going to go over to the hospital and see your grandfather, then we'll head home."

"I don't know that I'm ready to go back just yet," I said.

My father continued to stare at me. He kept his voice very even. "Well, you just get yourself ready, young lady."

"I'll have to see if that's what Grandpa wants—" I started to say, but the phone cut me off.

My father answered it.

"Oh, hi, Angela," he said. "This is Michael." Then there was a short pause and he said, "Yes." My dad was probably the last person she ever expected to answer her phone. "I came up to get Lucy." Then he explained that my grandfather was in the hospital. He was quiet for a while, and after they went back and forth a few times, he hung up.

My father was very tense driving over to the medical center. I knew he wanted to yell at me but he didn't say a word in the fifteen minutes it took us to get there. I didn't, either. I might have said I was sorry that I caused them to worry, but let's face it, he had caused me a lot of heartache the last few months.

My grandfather had spent an uneventful night, the nurse said. But his blood pressure was very high and they

were "concerned." My father didn't seem to have any reaction to that news. I was tempted to ask what *concerned*
meant, but since my father was there I didn't. He headed
down the hall in the direction the nurse pointed. He was
walking faster than usual—I stayed close behind him. I
wanted to see what my grandfather's reaction would be
when he saw his son.

My dad went right into Grandpa's room without
knocking. "I thought I might see you this morning," my
grandfather called out. He was sitting up in bed, finishing
a breakfast of rubbery-looking scrambled eggs and mushy
toast. He saw me looking over my dad's shoulder. "Party's
over," he said.

My father didn't turn around to look at me.

"Hi, Dad," was all he said. He paused for a second at the
end of the bed, then he went up to hug his father. It was
an awkward hug, and not just because it's difficult to hug
someone who's sitting in bed.

It was strange to hear my father call someone "dad." He
must have done it the last time we were there—I just hadn't
noticed it. It made him seem vulnerable or small or something. It was weird. I didn't like it.

"How you feeling?" my dad asked as he pulled a chair
up near the bed.

"I'm great, just ask Lulu." He smiled at me and I gave
him a little wave from back by the door. With my father

around, I seemed to have lost all my power, like Superman in the same room as kryptonite.

"Well," my father said to him, "apparently your blood pressure is still very high, so they may want to keep you here for a while longer."

"That's nonsense. My blood pressure has been high for years. I operate hot, that's all."

"Well, we can talk to the doctor." My dad seemed to be getting more tired by the second. "Angela called. I told her what happened—"

"You told Angela? What did you do that for? Now she'll just worry."

"She needs to know what's going on. She said she was going to change her plane and come—"

"Oh, no."

"Look, I've got to get Lucy back, and you should have someone with you." My grandfather was shaking his head, getting mad. I'm not sure if he didn't want to disturb his wife's trip or if it was just being near my father, but he wasn't happy.

The doctor came in and explained that high blood pressure was a primary cause of strokes, and since my grandfather had had a few TIAs, the smart thing would be to keep him in the hospital for another day, just to make sure everything settled back down.

"I'll go and get you some decent food." My father finally

broke the silence that had descended like a bomb on the room after the doctor left—he was itching to get out of there.

I stayed with Grandpa. Eventually he told me to get some money out of his pocket and go down to the vending machine to get myself a Coke. He only had a ten-dollar bill.

The vending machine was just outside the tiny gift shop that sold gum and candy and newspapers and small stuffed animals and a rack full of different road maps. I could understand everything else, but the maps seemed a little out of place. Is anyone going to go on a long-distance driving adventure straight from the hospital? The store also had a plastic bucket on the floor with several bouquets of flowers wrapped in that clear plastic. The arrangements weren't really very pretty—a bunch of fairly limp carnations mixed with some purplish things I'd never seen before—but at least they were flowers. My grandfather laughed when I came back with one of the arrangements. "Thank you very much, Lulu," he said.

My dad returned with some bagels and an egg salad sandwich and a newspaper. Then he left again to make some phone calls. "This is technically a workday for me," he grumbled as he walked out the door.

They took my grandfather's blood pressure every hour. "That's just making it worse," Grandpa complained, and I'm sure he was right. How can you relax when someone is coming in every ten seconds to check and make sure you're relaxed?

By the time we left him it was late afternoon. Time passed much faster than I would have predicted, considering that only two of the people in the small room all day were getting along with each other.

19

THERE WAS A MESSAGE FROM ANGELA on the old answering machine when my father and I got back to the house. She'd be home the next night; it would be late by the time she made it to Bennelton from Logan airport in Boston. My father wrote down Angela's flight number, drifted into the living room, and flopped down in a big armchair. The chair had a good view out the window, down the hill toward the sea. An empty coffee mug on a coaster was still where my grandfather had left it on the side table, next to a pile of magazines and newspapers. It was clearly my grandfather's chair.

"Are we going to head back home tomorrow, Dad?"

"We'll have to see how your grandfather is doing in the morning, but we might have to wait another day, till Angela is back." He looked around. When he realized where he was sitting, he stood up and shook his shoulders.

"I'm going for a nap," he announced. He had no interest in talking to me.

I understand that a lot of teenagers hate their parents, maybe for no real reason except that they exist and cramp their kids' style and are a hassle, and I've felt that way about my parents to a decent degree as well, but it was just normal teenager hate, nothing very deep or personal. Standard stuff. My parents just didn't get me very well, or properly appreciate me, which was fine, I was used to it. But now my relationship with my father truly sucked and was getting worse and it didn't seem like there was any hope of it reversing itself. Not that I cared all that much, but I did.

My father reappeared after his nap and we had BLTs for dinner, which under other circumstances might have been a tasty treat. But they just made me think of my mother. No one cooks bacon like my mom—perfectly crispy and without burning.

Once it got dark, fireflies started blinking on and off in the front yard. Last time we were here, Julie, my dad, and I went out and caught a bunch. This time I just watched them through the window. I'd gotten a little old for that kind of thing anyway, I suppose.

Upstairs, I tried looking at the moon through the

telescope. To my great surprise, it actually worked. The moon was just a few days before or after full, I couldn't tell which. I wonder how you can actually tell which it is—I've got to learn that. I got a good look at the man in the moon. He looked content, wise, happy. I could not relate at all.

I crawled into bed and stared at the cracks in the ceiling. I must have fallen asleep at some point because while it was still dark my father shook me awake.

"I've got to go to the hospital. Something happened to your grandfather. You stay here and sleep and I'll be back in a few hours. I just didn't want you to wake up and not know where I was." He must have been asleep too because his hair was all pushed up on one side and there was a crease down his cheek from his pillow. But he was wide-awake on the inside. His eyes, even though they were all puffy, were super focused.

"I'll go with you," I said, sitting up fast.

"No. Please, Lucy, just stay here. Sleep. I'll call you in a few hours and come back and we can go over then."

I listened to my father go down the creaking steps and out the front door and then heard his car crunch over the pebbles on the driveway. I lay awake until the sky started to lose its darkness and the birds began their morning chatter. When I went to the window, the cardinal was there on the branch just outside. I guess that was his spot after all.

By the time my dad called me at around ten in the morning, I was certain the news was going to be bad. It was. My grandfather had had another stroke. They'd taken him by ambulance from the small medical center to a larger hospital about forty-five minutes away. My dad was trying to be very calm and clear on the phone, but I could tell by his voice that he was kind of shaken up. He sounded young. He said he'd come back as soon as he could to get me, probably around noon or one.

"Can I go over and see Grandpa?" I asked him.

"We'll have some lunch and I'll take you over."

I was sitting on the front stoop when my father's car turned in the driveway. He got out slowly, walked toward me, and stood there. He looked like he needed a hug. But I just couldn't do it.

"Have you eaten anything?" he asked.

"Not really," I said.

"Well, let's find something." He walked past me into the house.

My dad made us omelets—there wasn't much left in the fridge besides eggs. Then he called my mom. The news was not good. They weren't sure the full extent of the damage at this point, but my grandfather had not regained consciousness. My father used the word "massive" to describe the stroke.

Grandpa was on the second floor in intensive care. There was a strong smell to the place: a combination of disinfectant, sweat, medicine, and something I couldn't place—maybe death. He was in a room full of beds, most with curtains pulled around the patients. I tried not to look at the ones whose curtains weren't closed.

Grandpa's curtain was open, and when I saw him from a few feet away, I stopped. I didn't mean to stop—I just did. I don't know what I had expected, but it was as if everything I had in my mind about how a sick person in the hospital would look was blown to smithereens—this was much worse. He was hooked up to about fifty machines and looked sunken in on himself. His mouth was open and hanging off to the right, his eyes closed. He looked like he might already be dead.

My father touched my shoulder, and we moved closer to the bed. "Come on, Lucy, let's sit down." He pulled up a chair beside the bed and stood behind it. "Hi, Dad. I've got Lucy with me here." He was talking like my grandfather was awake and could hear him. There was a lot of beeping from various machines in the room.

"Hi Grandpa," I said. My voice sounded very small. I turned to my father. "Can he hear us?"

"I don't know."

We only stayed a few minutes, then went to the cafeteria. My dad had a coffee and I got a Coke. We sat around a table in plastic orange chairs. My dad took one sip of his coffee, made a face, and pushed it away. Under the fluorescent lights he looked awful. His eyes were bloodshot, with dark, puffy circles underneath.

"You wait here. I'm going to go find the doctor. I'll be right back." He pushed back his chair.

I'd never really thought of my dad as old, but the way his shoulders slumped as he trudged away, I hardly recognized him.

As I looked around, everyone seemed exhausted. Private tales of heartache were everywhere. It took my father a lot longer to come back than he said it would. Somehow he managed to slip right in across from me without my noticing. He was quiet for a minute; I could tell he wanted to say something to me.

"Let's go see your grandfather again. Then we'll head home."

"Our home? You can go if you want, but I'm not going to leave Grandpa here all alone and head back to New Jersey."

"No, Lucy. To Grandpa's house. I just meant . . ." but he didn't finish the sentence.

I wasn't nearly as shocked to see my grandfather this time, but in a way it was almost worse, since I was able to take in the scene a little bit more. I could see where he'd missed a spot shaving under his jaw. How could this have happened so fast? How could life be so precarious?

I sat in the chair again and my father stood behind me. We didn't have much to say. After a few minutes my dad reached out and squeezed his father's hand.

"Careful," I said. "He's got a tube there."

"I see it, Lucy," he said. His voice was quiet. Then he looked at my grandfather, and whispered, "We'll see you a little later, Dad."

When we were in the car my father told me that Grandpa was in a coma.

20

ANGELA ARRIVED IN THE MIDDLE OF THE NIGHT. I woke up to find that my father had already taken her over to the hospital and would be back around noon to get me, same as yesterday. I learned all this from a note that my dad had left on the kitchen counter. Beside the note he had placed Grandpa's large box of Wheaties along with a bowl and spoon. "Rice milk in the fridge," said a P.S. at the bottom of the note.

I ate some of the stale flakes and wandered out front. I was looking up into the trees at some birds twitching around when Davis came out from his apartment.

He was in full action mode. He had shaved and said he'd switched shifts at work till later and was going over to the hospital to see my grandfather. Did I want a ride?

My dad and I had run into Davis the day before as we were returning from the hospital with the take-out pizza we had gotten for dinner. My dad had filled Davis in on the situation, and Davis reacted the way you would expect, which was basically with disbelief, confusion, shock, and then sadness that seemed to spread out around him. He didn't say a lot and he declined when my dad invited him to have pizza with us. I couldn't wait any longer and put the pizza box on the hood of my dad's car and took a slice. Then my dad grabbed a slice and then Davis took one too. We all just stood around the front yard eating pizza till it was gone, as the air around us got dark.

I hopped in his car. As we drove, Davis started telling me about how my grandfather had helped him out by giving him a place to live. "And he vouched for me at the fish-processing plant, even though he didn't know me from a hole in the head at that point. He said the only reason he did it was so that he could be sure I had a job so he knew he would get his rent." He tried to laugh at that. "But he went out on a limb for me."

It was pretty clear that Davis was still shaken up by what had happened and was in a rush to see Grandpa for himself. Both his hands clutched the wheel as he drove. Apparently Davis had been in drug rehab for a long time. He'd gotten in some legal trouble, too, and he had been trying to get himself sorted out.

"Every day I'm more grateful to that old man," he said to me. "I can't imagine what would have happened to me if your grandfather . . ." but he didn't finish the sentence.

When we turned into the hospital parking lot, he said, "To this day I have no idea why he did it."

They had moved my grandfather to another floor. The atmosphere here was even heavier than in the last place they had him, if such a thing was possible. You could feel it the second you got off the elevator. It was also much quieter: no buzzing or ringing machines, no one hurrying past with a clipboard and an urgent look on her face, no patients walking up and down the hallway in hospital gowns, stretching their legs, wheeling IVs beside them, no delivery boys with flowers scurrying this way and that.

Grandpa was in room 319—a single room. The door was mostly shut but Davis pushed it open with a soft knock. Angela was in a chair beside the bed and turned to look over her shoulder as we came in. My dad was standing on the far side of the bed.

"Lucy," he said.

"Davis was coming over anyway, so I hitched a ride."

"Thanks, Davis," my dad said.

"No sweat," Davis whispered. He was staring at Grandpa, who, if anything, looked worse than the last time I saw him. His eyes were still closed, his mouth still hung open at that weird angle, like he was screaming a scream out of the side of his mouth that only he could hear. He seemed to have sunk deeper into himself since yesterday.

Angela got up and hugged me. She said how much I'd grown up and all the typical stuff, which seemed rather weird considering where we were and what was happening, but I guess that's what people do—cling to the normal things to help them get by.

After a few minutes the three of us left Davis with Grandpa and went to the cafeteria. I wasn't very full. Both Angela and my dad looked pretty worn out. She had flown all the way from Germany and he basically hadn't slept in three nights. They each got a coffee and I had an OJ that was absolutely not fresh squeezed. Once we were sitting, Angela started to cry, then she stopped suddenly and got very still. At this point my dad had a funny look on his face pretty much all the time, as if he was just bewildered by life. We all just stared off, each in our own world. It's an interesting experience to space out when you're with other people who are spacing out as well. It's different than doing it alone. It was comforting.

When we got back to the room, Davis was telling Grandpa the story of how he had been arrested while walking down the street in his underwear with no idea how he had gotten that way.

Davis seemed kind of embarrassed when he realized we

were there. "It's his favorite story. I thought it might cheer him up a bit."

If it did, you sure couldn't tell. Grandpa hadn't moved a muscle. They say it's good to talk to a person in a coma, because we can't be sure exactly what they do and don't hear, so if it was Grandpa's favorite story, I was all for it.

When Davis had to head off for work, my dad suggested I go back to the house and hang out there; he'd be there in a few more hours.

As we were heading to the car across the parking lot Davis kept saying, "I just can't believe it, I just can't believe it." Davis had known my grandfather for just a little over a year, but Grandpa had such a big effect on his life. By now I had come to the conclusion that Davis was a really cool guy, very gentle. I was glad he had gotten himself straightened out—I guess my grandfather was a pretty good judge of character.

I stopped where I was in the parking lot, right before we got to the car. "Actually, Davis," I said, "I'm gonna hang out here."

When Davis drove away I felt very alone. I didn't go back in right away; I just wandered around outside the building. I plucked some small leaves from the shrubs lining the parking lot, then peeled them down the vein in their center. I used to do that a lot when I was a little kid, trying to get them peeled perfectly. It was an activity that took all of your attention and none of it at the same time. Some cars arrived, some left. I wondered if any people had died inside the hospital since I had gotten there a few hours earlier. I had never really been around death, and now it felt all around me.

Back inside I had to wait a long time for the elevator. When I finally got in, I went to push the third-floor button, but at the last second I saw the sign for the maternity ward on the fifth floor, and I pushed that instead.

Now this was a happy floor—a whole different world from the third floor. There were people smiling in the hallway, old people and young kids; folks carrying balloons, flowers, stuffed animals—there was a general happy energy. I acted as if I knew just where I was going, even though I had no idea, until at the end of the hall I found the room with the massive window where they keep the newborn babies. Six of them lay in little Plexiglas bassinets, all swaddled up. Four were asleep, one was screaming his head off, and the last one was staring off like a tiny, serious alien, maybe looking out through the folds of this plane of reality to that other realm, from whence he had just emerged. For some reason I thought about those stories you always hear about babies who are switched at birth. I hoped all these little guys had been tagged properly and didn't end up with the wrong parents, only to discover years later that there had been some mix-up, explaining why they alone had red hair in a family of dark-eyed Italians. Life is difficult enough without that kind of screwup.

A man came up next to me and practically pressed his face against the glass. I sneaked a peek at him out of the corner of my eye and saw that he had the biggest grin, and tears were streaming down his cheeks. The look of love. It was difficult, standing there in the presence of such unguarded adoration, to imagine how it could all get so far off track later on.

I wondered if my dad had gone to the hospital to see Thomas when he was born. Did he have tears streaming down his cheeks? What did he feel looking through the glass? I started to get angry at him all over again.

Eventually, I found the stairs and walked down to the third floor. The hallway was as quiet as before, the atmosphere just as heavy. Grandpa's door was slightly ajar. I thought I could hear my father's voice, whispering. I figured he was talking to Angela, but as I pushed the door, I saw that he was alone with my grandfather. I was about to announce my presence, but I stopped.

I couldn't exactly understand what my father was saying at first, but I definitely heard him say, "I'm sorry, Dad." The first part of the next sentence was lost to me as well, but it ended with, ". . . I couldn't be the son you wanted." I stayed back by the door. He said something about them not being a "good fit." He sniffled and then cleared his throat.

Was my dad crying? He cleared his throat, and I heard him say, "A lot of my best qualities come from you. You need to know that. I wish things had been different between us, but that doesn't matter anymore. It just doesn't matter." From behind, I could see him wipe his eyes. "It's all okay now," he whispered. "None of that matters." He breathed out heavily. "I love you, Dad," he said through the end of his sigh. Then he said it again. "I love you." He was rocking forward and back slightly now. He whispered something to my grandfather about not being afraid and that he was free. He said that my grandfather was clear, or something like that. He repeated that a few times, "You're all clear here, Dad, you're clear." I know I shouldn't have stayed and listened as long as I did, but I had never seen anything like it in my life.

All the anger I had felt for my father upstairs in the maternity ward was gone. I don't pray a lot but I asked God—if there was a God—to let Grandpa hear what my dad was saying. I crept back out the door.

I was standing in the hall when my father came out of the room a few minutes later. His eyes were red.

"Lucy," he said. "I thought you went back with Davis."

"Yeah." I shrugged. "I changed my mind."

"What have you been doing all this time?" He blew his nose into some tissues.

"Just hanging around."

"Let me find Angela. She went for some air. Then I'll take you."

"I'll hang out with Grandpa till you get back."

"Are you sure you're all right?"

"Of course. I'm not six."

"I know, Lucy. It's just . . ." He didn't finish his sentence. "You're right, talk to him. He'll like to hear your voice right about now, I'm sure."

I went in. The chair was still warm from my dad.

"Hi Grandpa," I said and waved at him. The other day we had been laughing and chatting about nothing at all, and now it was like he was already dead. I felt guilty thinking that, but I couldn't get it out of my mind. I didn't know what to do or say, and then suddenly I just started humming this song my mother used to sing me when I was a little kid. I couldn't remember the words at first, so I just hummed softly. Then in a rush all the words came back and I was singing, "As he strolled along, he sang a song of a land of milk and honey." I wasn't exactly belting it out the way Julie might, but I hoped Grandpa was enjoying it. "Where a bum can stay for many a day, and he don't need any money. Ohhh, the buzzzzzin' of the bees . . ." That was my favorite line. I could still hear the way my mother used to make a buzzing sound when she sang about those buzzzzzin' bees. I started to laugh at that and then I was crying at the same time. I was sad about Grandpa, of course, but also about my mother, and all those times when I was a kid and didn't realize how nice my life had been.

Angela planned to stay overnight at the hospital with

my grandfather, so my dad and I headed home. Since there was still nothing much at the house to eat, we walked into town for dinner. We tried the fish and chips place. The fish was not terrible, for fish, and the fries were delicious, firm and tasty. Night had fallen pretty hard by the time we were done. There were only streetlights on the corners once we got off the main street and we didn't have a flashlight. It got very dark very fast between the lights.

"Is Grandpa going to die soon?" I asked in the blackness.

"I think so, Lucy, yes," my father said.

It was not a surprise, given the way the day had unfolded, but still, the news hit hard. My dad had a difficult time getting through the sentence without choking up, and I had a difficult time not bawling right there in the gutter. I was glad it was so dark. When we got back to the house we turned on the TV for a while and then went to bed.

After a few hours I woke up. That was unusual for me. Sometimes it takes a long time for me to get to sleep, but once I'm out, I usually stay out till morning. The house was quiet and I just lay there in the dark for a while. That spot between my shoulders was at me again—feeling all vulnerable. But truth be told, I think all of me was feeling pretty vulnerable at this point. When a long time had passed and I was still wide-awake, I went out in the hallway and saw that a light was on downstairs, shining from the direction of the dining room or the kitchen. I started down the creaking steps, my hand on the banister.

My dad was sitting in the kitchen, at the table. He had a cup of tea in his hand.

"Lucy," he said. "What are you doing up?"

"I don't know." I shrugged and took one of the other chairs at the table, across from him. The floor was cold under my feet.

"Do you want a cup of herbal tea?"

"No thanks."

"It's funny," he said. "I've never been so tired in my life, and I just can't sleep."

Neither one of us said anything for a little while.

"Do you want some cereal? I think it's all we have. I've got to go shopping tomorrow."

"How long do you think we'll stay here?"

"I'm not sure, Lucy."

You could hear the cow clock ticking above the hum of the refrigerator.

"I want to thank you, Lucy."

"Me? For what?"

"If you hadn't come up here"—then he cut himself off and gave me a stern look that I wasn't sure was real or play. "And we haven't even talked about that yet." Then he relaxed again. "Then no one would have been here. With Angela away he needed someone. And now . . ." He shook his head a little. "It's been important."

He started to get choked up.

"I'm sorry," he said.

"Why? Don't be." It *was* a little weird to see my dad start to cry; it's not something I had a lot of experience with in my life, and now I'd seen it several times in a day.

"I'm surprised," he started to say, then he had to stop again. He took a deep breath and kind of shook his head. "I'm surprised how emotional I've been about it. I mean, we didn't exactly get along very well, and I hadn't seen him much, as you know."

"If you can't cry about your dad almost dying, what can you cry about?" I said.

My dad laughed. Then I laughed too. I hadn't intended to be funny, but I guess it came out that way a little. Then I burst out crying.

"Lucy, what is it?" He reached across the table toward me.

I leaned back, away from him. "I think it might be my fault," I said through my tears, which were starting to come fast and furious. Maybe it was his crying that had triggered mine, but this had been on my mind for days now.

"What is? What's your fault?"

"Grandpa's stroke." I started to breathe heavily. "Him going to die."

"How could that possibly be your fault, sweetheart?"

"He ate the ice cream." It was difficult to talk in sentences. "He told me . . . he wasn't allowed to eat any." I was almost hyperventilating now.

"Lucy, sweetheart, calm down. It's okay; what ice cream?"

My dad pulled his chair over and he had his hand on my back. "It's okay, just take a deep breath."

I tried to calm my breathing for a while. I was still crying hard. "We were at the restaurant and I had ice cream for dessert and he said that his doctor forbid him to eat ice cream anymore. That the dairy was bad for him. Well, he could tell I was disappointed."

"Why?"

"Remember when we came up here? We went to that ice cream place that night when it was raining and he ate that giant hot-fudge sundae?"

He smiled faintly "I forgot about that."

"Really? That's what I remembered most. I remembered how much he liked that ice cream, and the way it dripped on his chin and how you were so sweet and gave him a napkin."

My father nodded a little as if he were trying to remember.

"So I was looking forward to having some ice cream with him, then he said he couldn't, but then he could see how disappointed I was, so he ordered some anyway and ate it. Then he ate mint ice cream at the sushi place. I poisoned him. It was my fault." I was staring at my father now. My cheeks were soaked with tears. My dad was looking back at me.

"Shhh," he said softly. "Shhh. Lucy, now you listen to me. There is no possible way that eating a bowl of ice cream caused Grandpa's stroke. It had been building up for a long time. It's just one of those things that happen in life sometimes. You heard the doctor say how high his blood pressure had been. An ice cream he had with you had nothing to do with it. Believe me."

I guess I knew he was right, and now that I'd said it out loud it did seem kind of silly. But it sure had been messing with my head for a while. I leaned back away from my father and sat there for a minute, looking at my hands in my lap. I could tell my dad was still looking at me, but I couldn't look back at him. He got up and went to the bathroom and came back with some toilet paper. He gave some of it to me to wipe my face and blow my nose. He did the same with the rest.

"Well, look at us," he said standing over me. "A lot of snot." He kind of forced a chuckle, and I forced a little one back.

"Gross, Dad." And we both went up to bed.

When I woke up my room was very bright, and the birds were not singing nearly as much as usual. It must have been late morning. I found my dad at the kitchen table in the same spot he had been in the night before. At least his clothes were changed and he'd had a shower. My grandfather had died.

21

I HAD TO CALL SIMON. Suddenly it was urgent for me to hear his voice. I hadn't even been gone a week, but too much had happened. Part of me wondered if he'd already started to forget about me. Or at least give up on me.

He hadn't.

"Hey, hey-O!" he shouted into the phone. As naturally cool as Simon is, his goofy side was what I found most endearing. I've never been so relieved in my life to hear someone so happy to hear my stupid voice. I just started laughing.

"What's so funny?" he asked me.

Finally I had to calm down and tell him that nothing was funny, in fact, things were the opposite of funny—that I was shrouded in death up here in Maine.

Simon was super sympathetic. Both his grandfathers had died, so he knew something about what I was going through.

"Maybe I should come up on the bus," he said.

I could literally feel my heart slam against my chest, but I told him not to. I don't know why I said that, except that my parents would be there and I didn't think I could handle all that. Anyway, these next few days were about my grandfather.

Then Simon told me that he'd been back to Thomas's place. He liked how quiet it was over there and he'd gone to the park across from the apartment just to hang out.

"He saw me and came out with a boomerang."

"Did his mother know?" I asked.

"I guess. She called him from the window after a while."

"Was she mad?"

"I don't think so, why?"

Simon couldn't see me shrug.

"He started calling me the 'Sime-ster.'"

"The what?" I squealed.

"I know, right? He's a funny kid."

"If you say so."

"It was the first time I've ever used a boomerang where it actually worked. I chucked it and it circled around and came back to me. Not exactly right to me, but pretty close. It was very cool. Thomas is a pro at it."

For some reason I was glad that Simon had seen Thomas again.

My mother and sister were coming up on a flight the next morning. Meantime, my father had to drive Angela over to the funeral home to make arrangements. When they came back a close friend of Angela's named Monique was with them. Apparently Monique lived a few blocks away. Angela called her a spiritual sister. A few other people arrived at the house. Friends of my grandfather came by to see Angela and to try and understand what had happened so quickly. All day long there seemed to be some new person in the kitchen, leaning against the counter or sitting at the table—everybody shaking their heads, talking softly.

Everyone assumed my dad and I were just the relatives who had come up for the funeral. No one knew that I had been there, that I had been the closest person to my grandfather on those final few days.

At one point I slipped into the kitchen, opened the cabinet under the sink, and found a large green garbage bag. I went outside and picked up the rake that was still lying where my grandfather had tossed it down and gathered up the little piles of gutter glop we had left behind. I dumped them in the garbage bag and deposited it at the curb.

Back inside, an old man with the biggest, fullest head of white hair I had ever seen kept the coffeepot percolating—

that seemed to be his job, refilling everyone's cup. Davis hung out on the front stoop. He didn't come in at all, but he stayed there all day. Occasionally I went out to hang with him. He was very quiet. He didn't mention anything, but I think he was glad I came out as often as I did. My dad shook everyone's hand who came in.

It was a strange day all around. Time behaved very weirdly. I would glance at the clock and couldn't believe that only two minutes had gone by since the last time I had looked. I would swear it had been hours. Once, while a few people were at the kitchen table talking, I got up on a chair to check that the cow clock above the stove hadn't stopped, even though I could hear it ticking. I thought maybe the hands were stuck. Then later, one minute it was bright daylight and the next it was pitch-black night outside. I was glad to see the day come to an end.

In the morning my dad didn't even ask me if I wanted to drive to the small airport in Owls Head with him.

By the time he pulled back into the driveway with my mother and Julie, Monique was already at the house having coffee with Angela, and I was hanging around in the front yard, waiting, I suppose. Getting out of the car, my mother looked older than she had five days ago, but perhaps that was just the stress of everything.

We carried the bags into the house. My mom had brought me some clothes, thank God. She handed me the bag, but then didn't let go when I grabbed it. I looked up at

her. "We have a lot to talk about still, Lucy. Don't think because of this, that your running off is all done and forgotten."

"I know," I mumbled.

She let go of the bag and I went inside to change.
Angela had insisted we stay with her and I brought the bag
upstairs. People continued to come by the way they had
the day before, hanging out, talking and not talking. The
old man with the white hair took his spot at the percolator,
refilling everyone's coffee cup before they even asked. Julie
spent most of her time drifting in and out of the kitchen
where people were gathered, in her own world, almost as
if nothing was wrong. My parents sat in the kitchen greeting everyone.

The white-haired coffee man was shaking his head as
he refilled my mother's cup. "To think that I'll never see
Harold again," the man said to no one in particular.

"You think that's strange," I heard myself say. I was leaning in the doorway to the kitchen. "What about Thomas?
His grandfather just died and he never even got to meet
him. And now he never will."

Everyone turned to look at me.

"Who?" Angela asked. She also looked at me, confused,
standing over at the stove, warming up hot cross buns
someone had brought over.

I could feel my mother's and father's eyes on me.

"Thomas—" I started to say.

"Lucy," my mother cut in.

"He's this eight-year-old boy who lives near us."

"Please stop it, Lucy." My mother's voice was harsh now.

"Dad is his father and Grandpa never got to meet him." I was looking directly at Angela, but I could feel all the eyes in the room on me.

I'd had enough of the secrets, the lying. I was tired of everyone else dictating how things were going to go. But you could sure hear the cow clock tick in that kitchen. The room was silent.

"Please come outside, Lucy," my father said softly, and he got up. He had to turn sideways to squeeze past me in the doorway.

My mother eyed me with daggers as she stood up.

We left everyone in the kitchen and I followed after my dad through the dining room, then the living room and into the den where I had found the yearbook. Once the three of us were in there, my father closed the door softly.

"What exactly was the point of that?" he said.

"I don't know, I just think it's a shame that Grandpa never got—"

"Cut it out, Lucy," my mother scolded. "You did that deliberately to be hurtful toward your father."

"Well, ditto you to us, Dad."

"I never meant to hurt you, Lucy. I—"

"Too late for that one," I snapped at him. "You don't even care. You act like nothing happened—after all that we've been through."

"I care very much, Lucy, I have been trying—"

"Oh, spare me, Dad."

"You never betray our family like that, Lucy." My mother grabbed my arm as she lashed out. She was furious.

But that statement really made me laugh. "Are you kidding me!" I screamed. Then I turned on my father. "You betrayed everyone."

"Lucy—" My mother stepped toward me, but my father put his arm out to stop her.

"It's okay," my dad said. "Let her talk."

"This isn't fair. I didn't do anything and now I'm to blame. So typical. This sucks."

"Yes it does, Lucy, you're absolutely right," my father said. Then his voice was calmer. "It sucks. And it is my fault. I am very aware of that. And I hurt you, I am very aware of that, too. But we are here at your grandfather's funeral and we need to get through it and be respectful, if not to me, then at least to his memory. You are absolutely entitled to your feelings, but we need you to gather yourself for the next few days."

"Fine," I said at last. Then I started to walk toward the door.

"And nothing that has happened entitled you to run off like that, Lucy," my mother added.

"I couldn't take it anymore," I said, without turning around or even looking back at her.

"Take what?" she asked.

"Just . . . everything."

"That's ridiculous." My mother shook her head.

"It's not ridiculous," I said. I turned back to her, my face hot. "It was a totally insane thing to have happened. Dad has another kid, for God's sake! And you never even told us! How does that make any sense?"

"You're right," my father said. "I certainly could and should have handled it much better."

"You're always telling us to be honest and admit when we're wrong and all that crap, and it turns out that you're just one big lie! No wonder we're so messed up."

"Lucy." My mother had calmed down a bit. "I truthfully don't think we're that messed up."

"Oh, please."

The air settled around that comment. The afternoon sun was coming in through the one window and I could see the swirling dust motes, the same as when we had the discussion about Thomas in the living room back home.

"Is that the way you really feel?" my father asked. His voice was soft.

"I don't know." I shrugged. "Sort of. Sometimes. Yes."

No one said anything for a while, then my father started nodding his head to something only he could hear, just the way my grandfather had done. I never noticed that habit in my dad before, but now I realized he had always done it too.

"Okay, Lucy," he said softly. "We hear you."

"A lot of good that does," I mumbled. I didn't really need to add that; it was childish, I admit, and I could tell when I said it that I probably shouldn't have, but my parents let it go.

"We'll talk more about it later." He looked around the room and nodded again. "Shall we go back out to everyone?"

"At least I got to spend Grandpa's last days with him," I reminded them as my father went to open the door.

"You did," my father said. "And I'm proud of how well you've handled everything."

Just as I stepped out of the den I heard the front door slam. I guess my little announcement had sent a few of the guests packing. But right there in the living room, my sister was sitting all alone in my grandfather's chair, beside the stack of papers and magazines. She wasn't looking at us, and she didn't say anything, but I could tell she'd heard every word.

Later, when we were in bed, it was a different story.

The last time my sister and I had had to share a bed was when we had come up to Maine a few years ago—it wasn't as uncomfortable as it might seem. The night was cool, and we were under the heavy quilts. The telescope was by the window. The house was very quiet. It was one of the things I really liked about Maine—how quiet it became once everyone settled down.

We had been in bed for a while. I thought Julie was already asleep; she hadn't moved in a long time. I was in that space between being awake and asleep when I heard a voice. I was drifting and wasn't sure who was talking.

"I knew," the voice said.

"Huh?" I mumbled, then snapped back awake.

"I knew," Julie said again.

"Knew what?"

"About Thomas."

"What? How?"

"I heard them. Talking. I heard Dad tell Mom, years ago, when I was little. They were in the kitchen. They didn't know I heard."

The moon was out. I couldn't see it, but there was light coming into the room, and I could see Julie's face now. Tears covered her cheeks. I realized in that instant that I had almost never seen my sister cry. How could I never have noticed it before? She never cried, and now here she was, tears pouring from her eyes. She turned to me, and the dam really broke. She started sobbing, really sobbing. Her whole body started shaking so much that the bed shook with it. Seriously. She was convulsing—like she was having a seizure or something. She wasn't making a lot of sound— she was holding that in—but her face was contorted and the tears were flowing. I didn't know what to do. Finally, I reached out and grabbed hold of her and wrapped my arms around her as tight as I could. It seemed that if I didn't do that she would just shatter apart into a thousand pieces.

Finally, she started to calm down. She was still crying, but it wasn't so scary now. Eventually she caught her breath.

"Why didn't you ever tell me?" I asked her finally.

"I thought it would upset you," she said.

I laughed. "Well, you got that right."

Julie laughed at that too. Then her laughter turned into more crying, but not like before. After a while she was quiet.

The moon had moved across the sky and was coming into view out the window. It was nearly full—it had been getting bigger after all.

"You never told anyone that you knew?" I asked.

She shook her head and looked at me. Her eyes broke my heart. I saw how scared she had been, keeping her secret for so long. No wonder she never said much. I saw how relieved and how tired she now was. Then from deep inside Julie came a massive sigh, the biggest sigh I had ever heard, as if she was getting rid of a breath she had been holding for years and years. Which, I suppose, she had been.

"You won't tell Mom and Dad?" Her forehead was all scrunched up.

"Your secret's safe with me."

22

THE NEXT MORNING WAS THE FUNERAL. There was bright sunshine. Usually it's raining for funerals, or maybe that's just in the movies. I wouldn't really know; this was my first funeral. My mother had brought my dark blue dress. It felt good to be clean and dressed nice, even if it was under less than desirable circumstances. I was ready before everyone else and so I went out onto the front stoop to get some air. I was sitting on the top step watching the birds on the lawn when I heard someone call my name.

I looked up and there he was, striding up the driveway, goofy grin plastered across that beautiful face. Simon's long stringy arms swinging like they weren't attached to anything solid, and that wavy hair of his swooping across his forehead even more than usual. He looked like a movie star wearing a dark blazer, white shirt, and dark pants.

"Hi-ho," he said softly as he took me into his arms and kissed me—very heroic.

When we pulled apart he held me at arm's length, looked deep into my eyes, and said, "I'm really sorry to hear about your grandfather, Lucy."

In the midst of such a pool of sorrow I couldn't have imagined being happier.

My parents were as surprised as I was to see Simon, especially since they didn't know he existed. He was incredibly respectful to them. He said he was sorry for our loss and didn't want to intrude in any way. He had merely come up to see me and now that he had, he was fine to get the bus back home. I couldn't believe he could be so impressive in front of my parents. There was no trace of his awkward outsider persona. And it didn't seem like an act; it seemed like Simon, just Simon.

"Where do you live, Simon?" my mother asked him.

"New Jersey," he said.

"New Jersey?" my mom nearly shouted. I guess she had expected him to say "two towns over" or something like that.

"He lives a few blocks from us, Mom," I told her. "Simon is Maxine's brother."

"Oh," my mother said. She looked as if she were trying to

understand a foreign language. Her confusion was under-
standable enough, considering that a strange young man
whom she had never heard of had just traveled hundreds
of miles to see her daughter, only to say hello, and having
done so, was now content to leave. I suppose what she was
really doing was trying to compute that her daughter had
a boyfriend, and by evidence of the long trip just endured,
a fairly serious one.

My grandfather had never gone to church, but Angela
did every week, and so they were having the funeral where
she went. It was a modern kind of church, all wood, with
slanty angles. It was about a third full, with people scattered
around the pews. There was a skylight and a ray of sun was
shooting down at an angle, right onto the front row where
Angela, my parents, Julie, and I were sitting. The sun got
very hot until it moved along.

Angela must have mentioned to the priest some things
about my grandfather, because he told some stories, but
the man the priest was describing didn't seem a whole lot
like the man I had gotten to know. Maybe that's just what
Grandpa had meant—one person saw something or someone in one way, and another person saw that same thing or
person another way. Maybe it really was all in the way we
looked at things.

A few times during the service I looked over at my parents, who were gazing forward, holding hands. I'm not sure
they were even listening. My sister was on the other side

of them, fiddling with her hair. She had gotten up before me and we had not had a single second alone, so I hadn't spoken to her about the night before. But I have to say, Julie looked beautiful. Usually when I cry like that—not that I have ever cried like *that*, but when I have a big cry before bed—in the morning my face is puffy and my eyes are like slits. But Julie looked radiant—that's the only word for it.

I glanced over my shoulder and saw Simon a few rows back, next to Davis. He nodded to me and gave me a small smile. It was nice for everyone to just be in the same place, and be still for a while, thinking about my grandfather—or whatever else it was they were thinking about.

The graveyard was another story. Seeing the coffin and the hole in the ground—it was quite graphic. Not a ton of people from the church went to the graveyard, but those who did circled the grave. There was a large mound of dirt nearby under a blanket of fake grass. The priest was more solemn than he had been in the church. He didn't look up from his Bible as he read.

Pretty much everyone was crying to one degree or another, except my mom. She didn't shed a tear. I knew that look on her face; she was keeping an eye on everyone else, making sure we were okay.

When I glanced up I knew right where Simon was without even having to search—off to my left, standing in the back. His hands were folded in front of him and his head was down.

Two men in work clothes stood nearby. They were going to fill the hole with dirt once we left. After the priest finished, people slowly began to shuffle toward the waiting cars. It felt wrong just leaving Grandpa there. I understood that his spirit was gone, but what did we really know about it? I reached into my pocket and grabbed my three flattened coins. Before I turned to go, I tossed all three into the deep hole. I couldn't hear them land.

I had no idea what we were meant to do after that. How were things supposed to get back to normal after seeing a coffin being put in the ground? But Davis suggested we go to a place called Waterman's Beach Cottage. Apparently it was one of my grandfather's favorite places, and Angela liked that idea. So the caravan that had gone from the funeral to the cemetery set out again. The road to Waterman's Beach Cottage wound past rolling green fields that looked more like farm country than the rocky coast, but suddenly, there was the water.

We turned into a large gravel parking lot beside a crazy building that looked like two small shacks stapled together. With the sun shining and some small fishing boats out on the placid bay, it was quite a spot. A good many small islands were dotting the sea.

There were several picnic tables outside, and we took over the two closest to the water. A few people went to the window to order steamed lobsters, chowder, lobster rolls, a whole assortment of food. It felt strange, after all we'd just been through, to be getting on with such an ordinary thing as eating, But down there by the sea I felt like I could breathe for the first time in days.

The lobster rolls were really just fresh lobster and some mayonnaise crammed onto a regular hamburger bun. It didn't look that appetizing, but it was without a doubt one of the tastiest things I had ever consumed. The second was even better.

Then one of Grandpa's friends who I recognized from the house started laughing at something someone said. I felt like telling him to show some respect for the dead, but then someone else made a comment and the whole table burst into laughter, including my dad. I watched his face. I couldn't remember the last time I had seen my father laugh. Suddenly I could see that boy who had been staring out at me from that yearbook page, so alive and carefree. Even with the sadness of the day hanging on us, I felt glad to be alive, glad to be here with everyone. Especially Simon.

After a slice of delectable cherry pie topped with some homemade ice cream, while everyone was just relaxing in a way they never do back in the real world, Simon and I wandered off. We climbed down onto the rocks. They were pretty slick and barnacles clung to a lot of them. There was a real salty smell to the ocean. Simon picked up a long piece of seaweed and held it up in my face.

"Get that away from me," I shrieked. "It smells disgusting."

He laughed and threw it toward the water. When we

were around the point and out of sight from everyone, he kissed me. He had to bend way over to kiss me—he looked like a stork, like he always did when he was leaning toward me, and I was reminded of the first time he kissed me behind the garage.

While we were kissing, I opened my eyes and looked past his shoulder. The sun's reflection was shimmering bright on the surface of the water. Far out, I could just make out a fisherman leaning over the side of his tiny boat. A white seagull dove into the deep blue water. The wind blew. The air was the freshest I can ever remember breathing.

The lobster party went on long after any trace of the sun was left in the sky. That evening, my dad had stayed up talking with Angela. As far as I knew, he had never had much contact with Angela, but it was as if he was making up for lost time concerning my grandfather, or maybe he was just getting some more stuff off his chest.

Whatever they had talked about, the next day it was already near noon and there was still no sign of my dad.

"We're going to let him sleep as late as he needs to," my mother said. The original plan had been to get an early start and be home in time for dinner.

Simon had slept on the couch in the living room and planned to take the 9 a.m. bus, but my mom had insisted that he ride back with us.

"I'm sure they'll both really enjoy that," Julie said. Then she smiled at me in a way that was rare for her. She usually grinned without opening her mouth, but this was a full-on, toothy grin.

When my dad finally surfaced, my mom and Angela were making sandwiches for lunch.

"There you are," my mother said.

"I don't think I've slept that late in twenty years," my dad said. He kissed my mom and she put her arms around him.

"You okay?" she whispered.

"I'm good," he said, then kissed her again.

I'm not one of those people who believe in parents staying married for the kids and all that crap you hear about—those people who sacrifice their happiness for their children. They just end up resenting each other even more, and maybe resenting the kids, too, which obviously doesn't help anyone. But as I stood in the kitchen watching my parents kiss—something I have not done a whole lot of in my life—I was really proud of my mother. She had kept her eye on the bigger picture all the time. Not a lot of people could do that. I actually felt proud to be a woman myself— an almost-woman.

As my dad made his tea he looked at me. "Why don't you and Simon take the bus back together?"

My mother glanced up at him quickly. She didn't seem to think I noticed.

"Michael?" she said. It was nice to hear her call him by his name. She hardly ever did that; it was usually "darling" or "sweetheart."

He smiled at her—his blue eyes squinted. "They'll be fine," he said. "But we should go soon."

My dad was right. The only other bus of the day from Portland to Boston and beyond was at 3 p.m. It was an hour-and-a-half drive to Portland, so if we were going to make it, we needed to get a move on. After all that had happened, the goodbye to Angela and Grandpa's house wound up being a bit rushed, but that may have been for the best. Otherwise it could have turned into another day of lingering time and sad pauses. We all hugged Angela on the front stoop. I thought of the day I first arrived, when Davis and Grandpa had picked me up and we marched right over this stoop and into the house and then right back out again to go eat meatloaf in town. It seemed a million years ago.

All of us crammed into the car. I was squeezed up tight against Simon, which had its obvious benefits. Considering that it had taken me hours and hours from Portland coming in the other direction, the trip back to Portland was a breeze. The only problem was my parents pushing to get info out of Simon. They hadn't really gotten much of a chance to grill him until now. The fact that they were trying to be very casual made it worse.

"So, Simon, what's the name of the school you go to again?"

"Are you into sports?"

"Which ones?"

"You already thinking about colleges?"

"What did your folks say about you coming all the way up to Maine on your own?"

I wanted to throw myself under the speeding tires of the car. Simon looked at me out of the corner of his eye. I couldn't return his gaze. I was invisible.

"Mom," my sister finally said, "please." I looked over at Julie, who glanced back and shook her head. "Whatever," she mouthed.

For some reason that really made me laugh. Then Simon started laughing, and then Julie started. The three of us were guffawing it up in the back seat.

"What's so funny?" my dad asked.

"Nothing, Dad," my sister said, between laughs.

"I think we're too old, darling," my mother said to him.

23

I HAD IMAGINED SIMON and me taking that first-row seat on the bus, like I had on the way up, with the wide road in front of us. Instead, Simon walked right past the open front seat and kept going. By the time we arrived at the very last row I was reminded why I had fallen in love with this guy. He was a loner who liked to mingle—mostly with me.

Time was still playing its tricks, and the two hours to Boston seemed to go by in ten minutes. I think I spent most of that time singing the praises of Honey Dew Donuts. Simon had missed them on his way up. Once we got to the space-age bus terminal, we made a beeline there. I had two. Simon ate four. They were as good as ever. I watched as

Simon got that amazing glazed goo on his cheeks. I reached my hand over and wiped it off. He gave me his best goofy grin. This was one of those moments of pure joy—helping someone I loved discover one of life's pleasures, even if it was just donuts. I suppose that after the pain of death, the simple satisfactions taste sweeter.

Perhaps it's just buses that put me to sleep, or maybe it was the past week catching up to me, but I fell asleep on Simon's shoulder in the back row of the green Peter Pan bus as soon as we left Boston.

I woke up in Hartford, Connecticut, a few hours later. Simon said he had been just staring out the window, but it was dark now, and there was nothing much to see.

"I went back over to that park across from Thomas's house."

"I know, you said."

"But I went back again after I talked to you. I really like that park. There's never anyone there."

"Did you see him again?" I asked.

"Yeah. He came out with that bow and arrow and we shot it around for a few minutes. He asked where you were."

"What'd you tell him?"

"I said you were in a galaxy far, far away." Simon grinned at me. "But that you'd be back."

I reached up and kissed his cheek with a loud smack.

"What was that for?"

"Just because."

When we arrived back to that horrible Port Authority Bus Terminal, my father was waiting. We were quiet for most of the drive home. Then I just said it.

"Simon was with me when I went to see Thomas."

My dad looked over at me next to him in the front seat. Then his eyes shifted to the rearview mirror, where he could see Simon in the back.

"Were you," he said. It was more of a statement than a question.

"Yeah, I've met him a couple of times now," Simon said. "He's a nice kid."

My dad nodded that nod. I have to admit, The Nod looked good on him too. "I'm glad to hear that," he said, "that he's a nice kid."

We didn't say a lot more after that. Once we dropped off Simon, my dad spoke up. "When I saw Simon in Maine I assumed he was the one who'd gone with you to Thomas's house."

"How did you know I went there, anyway?"

"Because his mother called me."

"So you talked to her?"

"Yes, she called me. She saw a girl and a boy talking with her son and she asked him who they were and he told her that the girl's name was Lucy. She put the rest together."

"So she knows who I am, then?"

"She knows about you, yes. Of course."

"What's her name, anyway?"

"Oh, I'm sorry. Her name is Katharine."

"Was Katharine mad?"

"Mad?"

"That I was there."

"I wouldn't say she was exactly thrilled. She just wanted to know if I was aware that you were there."

"What did you tell her?"

"I told her the truth. I told her no, I wasn't aware."

We were both looking straight ahead as we drove.

"Was it nice to talk to her?" I asked.

"Lucy, it's not like that. We don't have that kind of relationship. We don't have any relationship at all. I've told you that."

"Yeah, but was it nice to talk to her?"

My dad shrugged. "It was, I suppose. It was nice to hear that Thomas was doing well."

"Do you think about him?"

"Of course I do, Lucy."

"Do you miss him?"

"Well," my dad said softly. "I've never gotten the chance to know him, so . . ."

A light ahead turned red and we slowed to a stop. When we weren't moving I could just barely hear my dad's classic rock radio station playing super low. Even at a whisper you could hear some guy screaming, "Dream on. Dream on. Dream on. Dream on. Dream on. Ooooo Oooo . . ."

"It must be hard for you?" I said.

My father turned to look at me. "It is, sometimes," he said. "But I brought that on myself."

"So are you going to talk to her again?"

"I don't know, Lucy. I mean, I'm sure I will, yes. We said we would talk soon."

The light changed and we started up again.

"About what?"

"I don't know. About Thomas, I'm sure. She just said, 'We'll talk soon.'"

"So it was Katharine who said it—'We'll talk soon.'"

"Um . . . yes, she said it." He glanced over at me.

"Well?" I said.

"Well, nothing. We'll just . . . we'll just have to wait and see."

We drove in silence for a bit, and then my dad looked over at me again.

"Simon seems like a nice fella," he said.

"Fella?"

"A nice guy. How's that? A nice young man. A nice person."

"He is," I said. "He's awesome."

My dad nodded. "I didn't even know you had a boy-friend," he said finally.

I shrugged. I'd been waiting for that one. "I guess you can never really know everything about a person, can you?" I said.

"Well, I don't know, Lucy." My dad seemed to be actually

trying to answer the question. "Perhaps not. But I suppose the best we can do is to try and let another person know who we truly are. To let them see *us*. That is, if we love them and trust them enough."

It had started to rain lightly. My dad shifted the wipers on slow speed. The pavement was shimmering a bit.

"And to do that," he went on, "we have to make an effort to reveal ourselves to them." He paused for a second before continuing. "I've been thinking a lot about this lately. My withholding the knowledge of Thomas prevented you from knowing me fully. And the reason I did that was because it showed me in what I thought was a bad light. And I'm truly sorry for that. It's my great loss that I shut you and your sister out like that. And your mother, too, for a while. I suppose that's why I told her when I did. I couldn't bear to have something between us that prevented our being closer. Even though it risked tearing us apart. And the only reason it didn't was because of the amazing person your mother is. I mean we went through a tough period, but I think we've come out the other side stronger."

I wondered if the reason my mom drank her wine every night had anything to do with what my dad had done.

"I felt the same about you and your sister," he went on, "but my shame and fear of what you would think of me prevented my telling you. I'm your father, you're supposed to be able to look up to me. I thought that you'd think poorly of me—that you'd hate me, and with good reason."

"I did," I said. "But even more because you never told us for so long. That made it ten times worse."

"I know," he said. "I just couldn't face the idea of you feeling that way—you thinking less of me."

"Maybe *you* thought less of you," I said.

My dad chuckled. "When did you get so wise?"

"I think it was somewhere around the New Hampshire border."

"And speaking of that," my father said, "there are going to have to be some consequences for your little adventure."

"It wasn't so little."

"No. It certainly wasn't. I don't mean to make light of it. I think it's a trip that will have some very far-reaching consequences for all of us. Nonetheless, you're grounded for a month."

I laughed. "Dad, do you hear how silly that sounds, after all we've just been through?"

"I do," he said. "But I'm still your father and I have a job to do and actions have consequences—"

"As we've all learned," I said.

My dad looked over at me. The rain had stopped. We turned into the driveway.

"As we've all learned," he repeated.

We were back home.

24

IT WASN'T SO MUCH that I gave my dad a wide birth after we returned; it was more that there now seemed to be a space between us, a distance that hadn't been there before. Without my anger at him filling the void, I could feel an absence—whatever it was. I knew things now, about my dad, about myself, that couldn't be unlearned. It wasn't necessarily a bad thing; it was just different. But he was still my dad, he would always be my dad, no matter what he did or I did. That was that.

My sister had her big end-of-summer musical. This particular one was pretty good. It was about a girl in an

English school who was hated by all the teachers and took her revenge on them. Usually when my sister was in one of her musicals, she paraded around the house singing all the time she wasn't at rehearsal, making a lot of noise, but that's about all you really got from her. But once we were back from Maine, she was different. I hardly remember her performing around the house at all, and she didn't race up to her room after dinner to listen to her show tunes. Instead, she hung out more. She came to my room and didn't irritate me as much. She talked about other things besides her show. She just seemed to be present in a way she hadn't been before. She was actually a pretty cool kid to be around.

She wasn't the main girl in the musical, just one of the classmates in the chorus, but honestly, Julie would have been much better than the girl they had chosen. Even from the back of the stage, you could see her sparkle. Simon agreed with me. Say whatever else you want about my little sister, but when it comes to the theater, she's got it. She truly does.

I missed my grandfather. I suppose that's a strange thing to say, since I met him twice, and only for a few days. I prefer to think that I knew him briefly, but well. Whatever it was that led me to seek him out, perhaps I'll never fully understand. I can only say that I'm glad I did. Meeting him when I did meant a lot to me.

Truth be told, I missed the adventure of the road too. If so much can happen in such a short time, then what are we doing with most of our lives, just going on from day to day with so little variation and excitement?

One afternoon when Simon and Maxine were away on a family vacation—in Utah of all places—I made a detour over to the park outside Thomas's house. I wasn't sure why, but I suppose I had known since we got back that I was going to go over there sooner or later.

I had planned to just sit on the bench across from his apartment building, like I had done the first time I saw him. But when I turned the corner Thomas was already in the park, playing with a small remote-control electronic helicopter. He was having some trouble getting it to fly correctly, and when he did get the thing up in the air, it was nearly impossible for him to control. From a distance I watched as it crashed into trees, then slam to the ground. I would have been much more aggravated by this than he was. Instead of being frustrated, Thomas laughed every time the contraption went zipping off into a nearby tree trunk.

Eventually he spotted me. He appeared happy enough, but really he just seemed to take my presence for granted, the way kids do.

"Do you know how to do these things?" he asked.

"No," I told him.

"Where you been?" he asked me.

"On the road to discovery," I said.

"Huh?"

"Nowhere much."

He let me have a turn at the helicopter, but I was no better at making it behave than he was. When I slammed it into the ground trying to circle a tree, he laughed. Then when the propeller came off, he just shrugged.

His mother came out from their apartment building. She was prettier than I remembered. Her hair was down and she had on a nice skirt. I suppose she was still in her work clothes—whatever her work was.

"Come on, Thomas, we have to go," she called.

"I just gotta fix this propeller."

"Now, Thomas." Katharine took a step closer to us, but stayed on the other side of the street.

"Mom, just hold on; if I don't fix it, it'll be broken."

"Go on, Thomas," I said to him softly.

"This is Lucy." Thomas pointed at me.

Katharine took a step closer to us, but stayed on the other side of the street. She just said, "Hi, Lucy."

"Hi," I answered. I didn't realize I had been holding my breath.

A car turned down the street and drove between us with its radio blasting. It went all the way to the circle at the end of the road and swung around. We watched it head back out toward Prospect Avenue.

"A wrong turn," Thomas said.

"We should get going, Thomas," his mom said. "We need to go and get back for dinner."

"Aw, Mom, I'll just wait here. Lucy can stay with me."

"Come on, Thomas," she said, moving to get into her car.

"Mom." He didn't budge.

"Now, Thomas."

"You know," I heard myself say, "if you ever do need babysitting, I'm pretty free these days."

His mom stopped. "Oh, well, thank you, Lucy," she said. She opened the door to her car.

"Yeah, Mom," Thomas said. "Like now."

"Not now, darling, but sometime maybe Lucy can babysit. Maybe on a Tuesday afternoon, when I have to work late."

I decided to help her out and demonstrate some childcare skills at the same time. "We'll do it some Tuesday, Thomas. But you go on with your mom."

"All right," he said, and then he stopped at the curb, looked both ways, and raced across the street. He was a pretty well-behaved kid. When his mother was halfway into the car, she stopped, stood back up, and turned back toward me. I was standing on the far curb with my toes dangling off the edge, like I had been that time with Simon.

"Actually," she said to me, "why don't you give me your number? You never know." She reached into her purse and started digging around.

"Okay." I stepped out into the street and crossed over toward her.

"Hold on a sec," she said as she pulled out her phone and started fiddling with it. "I'm not near as fast as you kids

are with these things. All right, there." She started typing.
"Okay, Lucy. Go ahead." Then she looked up at me.

Thomas's mother had startlingly blue eyes. I guess I just
hadn't been close enough to notice them before. Between
those gorgeous azure things and my father's pale blue ones,
there was no way Thomas was not going to have inherited
his enviable peepers.

After a few seconds she looked down and started typing
again.

"Your number?"

I told her, and she punched it in, stabbing at the phone
with the index finger of one hand the exact same way my
own mother did it, the same way I was always telling her
not to—she needed to use her thumbs, I always said; that's
the way it was designed.

When she was done she dropped the phone back in
her bag. Thomas was still standing by the car but he got in
when his mom did.

"See ya." He waved as he pulled the back door closed.

I watched the car back out onto the street, swing away
from the curb, and disappear as it turned onto Prospect
Avenue. I figured it was the last I'd see of them.

I was wrong.

A few weeks later, right at the end of summer, my phone
rang. I did something I hardly ever do when I don't recognize a number—I answered it.

"Lucy?" the voice said.

"That's me." I was a little leery.

"This is Katharine Eaves. Thomas's mother."

It took longer to respond than I intended. But finally I managed to get something out.

"Oh," I said—cloquent, right?

"How are you?"

"I'm good. I'm just hanging around in my room."

"Oh, that's nice. I'm sure it's a lovely room."

"It's not, actually," I blurted out. "I mean, it's totally fine. It's just not anything all that special." I didn't know why I was saying all this.

"So, Lucy," she went on, "you still up for a little babysitting?"

"Oh," I said again. I realized I had still been expecting her to yell at me. "Sure, no problem."

"Great, Thomas would enjoy that. How's next Tuesday afternoon?"

I told her that next Tuesday afternoon was fine.

"Do you know where Lincoln School is?"

"I went to school there."

"Oh," she said. "Of course."

There was a short pause that I had no idea how to fill.

"Well, Thomas is just finishing up his basketball day camp, so . . ."

"Got it," I told her.

"So if you'd just pick him up and take him back to the apartment for a few hours until I get home, that would be great."

"I can do that," I told her.

"Do you need to ask your parents if it's all right?"

"No, that's fine," I assured her. "They're good."

"Okay," she said. "Then I guess we're all set."

She asked if I had her phone number and I told her that I did; it showed up when she called.

"Oh, of course," she said, and sort of laughed a little.

I told her I'd text her after I had retrieved Thomas and we were on the way back to their place.

"That would be perfect," she said.

The following Tuesday I waited outside Lincoln School. I hadn't been back there since I graduated. I suppose it should have felt strange that Thomas was going to my old school, sitting in those same beat-up desks that I had, drinking from that same grungy low water fountain on the second floor that I used to drink from, but somehow it didn't. He gave me a big wave as he came through those big metal doors. I texted his mother and we headed back toward his home.

Thomas and Katharine lived up on the second floor. You entered into a big room, a combination living room, dining room, and kitchen. Four windows overlooked the street and the park beyond. Thomas wanted to practice his dribbling skills in the parking lot outside, and had to go to his room to get his basketball. "I'll be right back," he said, and ran through one of the two closed doors at the far end of the apartment.

"Okay," I called after him. "Take your time."

The place had a nice feel. It was neat and clean, but not fussy. It was a place where people lived. There was a huge couch that looked like it would be comfortable to fall into and watch a movie, with a large, squishy ottoman in front of it. The art on the walls was nice, but nothing fancy—a painting of fields and flowers, and an old poster for a movie with Charlie Chaplin, whoever he was. A black-and-white photograph showed a man kissing a woman; her head was thrown back, and he had a cigarette between his fingers. They were in a European city, maybe Paris—it had that kind of feel. Between two windows there was a full book-shelf. It wasn't in perfect order, but the books looked like they'd been read, or at least looked at, recently.

I walked back to the kitchen area, past a small table with one wooden chair on each side, and took a glass from the open shelves. I filled it at the sink—I didn't want to open the refrigerator. I took a huge swallow of water and wandered toward the view. I glanced out the window, exactly the way Thomas's mom no doubt had done to keep an eye on him, the same window from which she must have first spotted me. My gaze drifted to the bookshelf beside me and I caught sight of a tall, thin hardcover book. I couldn't believe my eyes.

That's a ridiculous expression, I know, but in this case it was true—I actually couldn't believe it and had to pick up the book to make sure. It was the same one I had as a kid, about the Japanese farmer. Their copy looked as well read as mine. I flipped through it to take a look at the paintings, but then I started to read.

The story was about an old farmer whose horse ran away one day. His neighbor came over to offer condolences. Such a thing was very unfortunate, the neighbor said. The old farmer nodded his head slowly and replied to him, "Maybe." The next day the horse returned, bringing with him two wild stallions. The neighbor saw this and came over to congratulate the farmer on such good luck. "Maybe," the old man replied. The next day the farmer's son climbed up on one of the wild horses and was thrown off and broke his leg. The neighbor came by to offer his sympathy. "Such bad luck," he said. "Maybe," the farmer answered. The day after that, the army came to draft all the healthy young men to fight in the war. When they saw the farmer's son with his leg in a cast, they didn't take him and went on to the next village. "What good luck," cried the neighbor. "Maybe," said the old farmer. And that was it.

I never really understood the story all that much when I was little. Maybe it wasn't actually a kid's book.

Outside, Thomas wanted to work on dribbling between his legs and behind his back. He started to walk from one end of the paved area to the other, bouncing the ball between his legs with each step. My job was to count each successful pass through his legs until he messed up—a typical boy's sports game. At first he made it three steps before he kicked the ball. Then he got up to six, then ten, and then eleven. He got to nineteen three times but couldn't break the twenty mark. He was really concentrating, I had to hand him that. Then in one turn he got a good rhythm going, I could tell right from the start. I counted along.

". . . eight, nine, ten . . ."

You could see he felt it too. He started to grin.

"Concentrate," I called to him. ". . . thirteen, fourteen . . ."

He was slapping the ball back and forth with authority now. The smile was gone. He was the picture of focus.

". . . sixteen, seventeen . . ." I must confess, I started to get really excited. It was just a stupid game, but damn, he was going for it.

". . . eighteen, nineteen, TWENTY . . ." I shouted out.

He kept dribbling. He got to twenty-five, then thirty. He got to thirty-seven before he kicked it.

"AW!" he yelled. But he was thrilled.

"Thirty-seven!" I shouted.

We both jumped toward each other and slapped a direct hit high five. It made a sharp, satisfying snap. I'm not sure who moved first, but we leapt into a quick hug. He squeezed me pretty hard with a little grunt; my arms wrapped around his sweaty little back for a second before we let go.

I hadn't felt this childishly happy and satisfied since I don't know when. My face hurt from my grin.

The late-summer sun shone down on us. There was a slight breeze moving through the leaves on the trees. Thomas was now trying to twirl the ball up on his fingertips. It kept falling off after less than a second. He was going to need a lot more practice to get any good at that. When the ball spun off his finger, it bounced away from him. He had to chase after it almost to the curb. When he looked up he saw someone—someone I had seen just a second earlier—come striding up the road.

He was back.

"Hi-ho!" Simon called, waving both of those skinny arms over his head like he was signaling for a ship from a desert island.

"Hi-ho!" Thomas called back. He ran to Simon and gave him a high five. Then he turned to me. "It's the Sime-ster."

Both Simon and I laughed.

Maybe having a little brother wasn't the worst thing in the world.

Maybe.

ACKNOWLEDGMENTS

Text TK